THE STOOGE CHRONICLES

The Stooge Chronicles

Commemorating the Golden Anniversary
of America's Favorite Comedy Team

JEFFREY FORRESTER

A Triumvirate Production

Contemporary Books, Inc.
Chicago

DEDICATION

For my good friends Dick and Abby, without whose help and encouragement this book would never have been possible.

ACKNOWLEDGEMENTS

Special thanks to Bill Cappello for research assistance, Earl Lord for access to his memorabilia collection, and Babe Howard for use of her photograph collection.

Thanks also to John A. Barbour for organizational consultation, Michael Bimmerle for promotional assistance, and Robert Dorn for his contribution of original artwork.

And, most importantly, sincere thanks to the many people whom I interviewed during the research of this book.

ABOUT THE AUTHOR

Jeffrey Forrester, a native of the Chicago area, is a graduate of Northern Illinois University. He received a Bachelor of Arts Degree in Journalism.

Introduction

The story of the Three Stooges is the story of a show business legend.

Despite the fact that they don't appeal to every audience, the Stooges have proved themselves to be one of the most popular, certainly the most prolific, comedy teams in movie history. They mastered the art of farce, developed a completely original style of comedy, and made more movies than any other comedy team in Hollywood.

Yet many film critics continue to dismiss the Stooges as ''minor'' comics, refusing to acknowledge them for what they really were: talented men who were capable of turning out great comedy.

This year marks the Golden Anniversary of the Three Stooges. Fifty years ago, they walked out onto a vaudeville stage for the first time as an independent comedy team, convulsing audiences with their slapstick antics and corny verbal humor. As Moe Howard pointed out years later, they never changed the content of their act. Perhaps this was the secret of their enduring popularity.

Their popularity is such today that one might assume the Three Stooges are in the midst of a cult revival. Their comedies are still among the highest-rated programs on the syndicated television market. Theaters across the nation continually book Three Stooges comedies for matinee and midnight showings, and Stooges film festivals can be found in every large city and college campus in the country.

Perhaps the reason for the Stooges' ''cult'' popularity is that their comedy is, in a sense, timeless. Despite the archaic settings and topical references often prevalent in their films, the comedy itself remains undiluted. In a nutshell, what was funny then is still funny today.

It is doubtful, however, that the Three Stooges will ever be remembered as one of the ''great'' comedy teams. They did not master the film art, nor did they attempt to do so. They simply used film as a convenient medium for presenting their style of comedy.

And for the memorable comedy they produced, the Three Stooges deserve at least a little applause.

I hope this book serves as an accurate evaluation of their career, as well as a modest tribute to the comedians who helped make my childhood a happy one.

JEFFREY FORRESTER

Contents

A Legend
of Comedy

Chapter One

Perhaps the most underrated and critically overlooked comedy team in the history of film-making is the Three Stooges.

The Three Stooges developed a brand of comedy uniquely their own. They specialized in a wildly violent style of slapstick, and produced a number of comedies which are now becoming recognized as classics of the genre. During their prime moviemaking years, the 1930s and '40s, the Three Stooges churned out a top-notch series of comedies, characterized by clever writing, inspired direction, and a fine cast of supporting players.

Film students have often pondered the reason for the Stooges' enduring popularity. Perhaps one reason is that, by physical features alone, the Stooges appeared to be living cartoons. This theory has long been held by Jules White, who produced and directed more than half of the Stooges comedies. Indeed, the cartoon-like action of their films (wild sight gags, exaggerated sound effects, and so forth) perfectly complemented their cartoon- character appearances.

Another fascinating aspect of the Stooges' comic personalities is that they represented the very bottom of the social ladder. Edward Bernds, who wrote and directed many of their comedies, believes their crude behavior was actually the basis for much of their appeal. "The kids can look at them and feel superior," says Bernds. "That's true of almost all comics. They all have some failing that makes you feel a little bit superior to them."

But even though the Stooges were indeed a "unique" comedy team, and have a significant number of quality movie comedies to their credit, they have been decidedly neglected by film critics throughout the years. The fact that they indulged in physical comedy and blatant verbal humor has damned them from most, as critic Leonard Maltin has put it, "respectable" film surveys.

While the Stooges rarely received critical acclaim—let alone acceptance—the moviegoing public loved them. This theory is supported by the fact that the Three Stooges comedy series lasted longer than any other in movie history. Jules White recently offered his personal evaluation of the Three Stooges as comedians:

"I think that in their line they were great. When you talk about Charlie Chaplin, for example, you're talking about the diamond of diamonds. Nevertheless, I've seen some of the Stooges films get bigger laughs than the same amount of footage of Chaplin's. Although Chaplin's were probably done with more finesse, that didn't necessarily make them any better. Because when you're after laughs, you're after laughs no matter *how* you get them. When you hear an audience shriek so loud you can't hear dialogue for a hundred and two hundred feet at a time, you can't ask for more than that."

Character comedian Emil Sitka, who appeared with the Stooges in many of their movies, points to their unique brand of comedy as the reason for their success.

"For farce, for split-second timing, they were great," says Sitka. "You take three other comedians and let them try to do the same things the Stooges did, and you'd see how hard it would be for them to do it."

Indeed, the Stooges' greatest comic asset was their timing, polished from performing almost exclusively before live audiences in vaudeville for more than a decade.

The Three Stooges received much of their training as part of an act called "Ted Healy and His Stooges." Ted Healy was a stand-up comic who formed the act in the early 1920s, and he used the Stooges as "second bananas" in both stage and screen appearances. The act was freewheeling and spontaneous, and improvisation accounted for much of the comedy.

The Three Stooges left Healy in 1934, and were signed by Columbia Pictures that same year to star in a series of movie comedies. The Columbia "Three Stooges" series lasted twenty-five years. These films were "short subject," or "two-reel," comedies, all of which were less than twenty minutes in length. During their tenure at Columbia, the Stooges starred in nearly two hundred "shorts," the last of which was released in 1959. The Stooges currently hold the record for appearing in more movies than any other comedy team in history.

The boss of the Three Stooges throughout its existence was Moe Howard. Born Harry Horwitz in 1897, Moe grew up in Brooklyn, and found work as a youngster playing child parts in silent films. Moe eventually graduated to traveling theatrical troupes, which exposed him to everything from vaudeville to the classics. Moe married Helen Schonberger in 1925, shortly before becoming a permanent member of the Stooges.

The "middleman" of the team was Larry Fine. Born Louis Feinberg in 1902, Larry grew up in Philadelphia, and, like Moe, pursued a show business career at an early age. He played child parts in vaudeville comedy sketches and eventually formed his own musical act. He started out with an act called "Fine and Dandy," and later teamed with the singing Haney Sisters. It was during his association with the Haneys that Larry met his wife, Mabel Haney. Larry became one of the Stooges in 1925.

The most popular member of the team was Curly Howard, Moe's younger brother and the patsy figure of the trio. Born Jerry Horwitz in 1903, Curly also had his share of vaudeville experience prior to joining the Stooges. Curly had appeared as a comedy conductor with a traveling band before joining brother Moe and Larry Fine as "Third Stooge." Curly was married, and divorced, several times through the 1930s and '40s.

Curly was eventually replaced in the act by another brother, Shemp Howard, then Joe Besser, and finally Joe DeRita. All three of these comics also had considerable vaudeville experience prior to becoming members of the Stooges.

As essentially "visual" comedians, perhaps the most significant physical aspect of the Stooges was their use of comic haircuts to accent their stage personalities.

Moe, the bullying, mug-faced "brains of the outfit," was known for his sugarbowl haircut, giving him the appearance of a walking spittoon. In a *New York Post* article on the Stooges in the late 1930s, reporter Michel Mok described Moe as the "dark, beetle-browed customer, the one with the bang on stage and screen." Mok noted that Moe was the Stooge who handed out all the "bangs" to his partners as well.

Larry permitted his naturally frizzy hair to form a bushy ridge around his head, complementing his character of the "Middle Stooge," whose sole purpose, basically, was to get in the way of his partners. Mok said that Larry's Aztec profile and frizzly hair made him look like "a malicious cartoon" of Leopold Stokowski.

Curly, whom Mok described as resembling "a lovesick stevedore," shaved his head; this, combined with his youthful facial features, gave him the appearance of a chubby little kid. Curly had a full head of hair and a moustache before joining the Stooges, but he shaved everything off upon his induction into the trio.

Curly suffered a series of strokes throughout the 1940s, and was replaced in the act by his older brother, Shemp Howard. Shemp, the oldest of the Horwitzes (he was born in 1895), had been with the Stooges in vaudeville, but had left the act to go out on his own in the 1930s. He returned to the trio after Curly became ill, and remained with the Stooges for almost a decade. Shemp wore his hair parted in the middle, and, like Curly, played the patsy of the group. But Shemp's style of comedy was on the opposite end of the pole from Curly's; he created a character that was diffident, yet decidedly flippant. Shemp's facial features were also an important part of his comedy. His squinty eyes, bulbous nose and elephantine ears qualified him as the "perfect" visual comic.

Shemp died in 1955, and was in turn replaced by Joe Besser, a chubby character comic. Besser was bald except for a horseshoe fringe of hair ringing his head, and, like Curly Howard, was rotund and cherubic. Several films that had featured Curly and Shemp Howard were remade with Besser. Often old footage of Curly, filmed in long shot, was passed off as new footage of Besser. Besser left the act in the late 1950s, after appearing in only a handful of comedies with the Stooges.

The final member of the Stooges was Joe DeRita, called "Curly Joe" because of his physical resemblance to Curly Howard. DeRita was also portly and wore a crewcut, playing up his physical similarity to the "original" Curly to the hilt. He remained with the Stooges until the act disbanded in the late 1960s.

These six performers constituted all of the various members of the Three Stooges. Other "Three Stooges" ensembles, however, popped up throughout the years, including a trio consisting of three other Healy Stooges, and another group that simply called itself the "Three Stooges." Strangely enough, both of these other teams also made movie appearances of their own at different studios. But of all the various groups, only the Columbia "Three Stooges" ensemble has received worldwide recognition as the ":legitimate" trio.

Through their physical appearances, the Stooges carried the tradition of silent comedy into the television age, even though they never made a silent film. Like the farcical clowns of the silent era, the Stooges maintained their oddball haircuts and appearances almost consistently throughout the team's existence. This, of course, helped establish their "removed from reality" look, a factor inherent to the farce of silent comedy.

Although they developed most of their comic skills in vaudeville, more than one film historian has noticed the similarity between the Stooges' slapstick nonsense and the antics of several silent film comics. The Three Stooges produced more variations on the single theme—sheer physical abuse—than any other comedians in movie history. They made famous such staples of low comedy as the "triple slap" (in which each Stooge receives a slap across the face in one swift blow), and the "poke in the eyes" (in which one receives two extended fingers in what appears to be the eyes). Through a fast-paced barrage of violent slapstick and rapid-fire dialogue, the Stooges perfected a successful pattern of popular comedy, often equalled by imitators in accumulative violence but seldom surpassed in style and underlying technique.

Violence was, however, the foundation for a great deal of Stooges comedy. Moe's constant physical abuse of his partners became a fixture in every stage and screen appearance the Stooges ever made. Ed Bernds describes how Moe was able physically to "punish" his partners without really inflicting pain.

"Moe had a knack of really slapping, but not hurting," says Bernds. "It was a trick of not having your fingers stiff. But it would still be a crisp slap."

The "poke in the eyes" was accomplished by quickly jabbing the fingers somewhere near the "victim's" eyebrows. If done quickly enough, and sound effects were added, the results were remarkably convincing.

Sound effects accounted for much of the Stooges' screen comedy. Moe's "painless" facial slaps were amplified through the magic of the sound effects department. Ed Bernds, himself a former sound technician, recalls that a violin or ukelele plunk was used to simulate the "poke in the eyes," while various percussion instruments were utilized for punches in the stomach and similar physical attacks.

Some of the Stooges' comic abuse turned out to be more than mere sound effects. Their stock-in-trade violence and the elaborate gags involved often resulted in near-disaster.

"The boys were always in danger of getting hurt," says Bernds. One of the worst on-the-set mishaps Bernds ever saw happened during the shooting of a Columbia Stooges comedy he was directing. The script called for a gag in which a bazooka gun was to backfire and shoot soot into Moe Howard's face.

"The special effects man used too much air pressure," says Bernds. "It blew off so hard that, even though Moe had his eyes closed, the soot shot up under his eyelids. Jesus, we thought he was blinded for life! The first aid man had to pry open Moe's eyes and actually took chunks of that black powder out of his eyes."

Moe Howard, the "brains" of the Three Stooges.

Shemp Howard, once named the "Ugliest Man in Hollywood," at age thirty.

Larry Fine received his share of physical abuse as well. In one comedy, a gag called for a fountain pen to be thrown into the middle of Larry's forehead. The pen was to be thrown on a wire and into a small hole in a tin plate fastened to Larry's head. But because of a miscalculation on the part of the special effects department, the point of the pen punctured Larry's skin, leaving a bloody gash in his forehead.

And Curly Howard had his troubles, too. Bernds was working as a sound man on a Stooges comedy in the late 1930s when he witnessed a bizarre gag that almost spelled disaster for Curly.

Tied to a spit over an open fire, Curly was "roasted" by his partners in an effort to thaw him out after he had fallen asleep in the back of a refrigerated truck. "Curly was so heavy Moe and Larry couldn't turn the crank," says Bernds. "The straps holding him slipped and he was hanging directly over the fire. Before they could get him off, he was pretty well seared."

Apparently Curly, who weighed more than two hundred pounds, was too heavy for stage hands to lift off the spit. As they struggled to get the straps loose so Curly could get off, they in turn were getting singed by the flames.

"Curly was hollering his head off, and I don't blame him," says Bernds. "Being roasted alive belongs to the Inquisition—not to making two-reelers!"

By the time Curly Howard retired from the act, many of the more elaborate sight gags had been eliminated from the Stooges comedies due to increasing production costs and decreasing production budgets. As a result, there was considerably less chance for injury to the Stooges themselves.

In life as well as in the act, the Stooges were distinctly different personalities. Moe Howard has been characterized as a tough businessman, not one to clown once out of costume and character. Ed Bernds points out an interesting relationship between Moe's comic character and his offscreen personality:

"Believe it or not," says Bernds, "in real life it was very much like it was in the pictures. Moe was the boss, the brains of the outfit. Larry used to take a beating; Moe kind of domineered him. Moe was really a sensitive, touchy guy, compared to the others. And his feelings were easily hurt, too."

Moe has also been described as a distant man, almost an introvert. Comedian Mousie Garner, who knew all of the original Stooges and was himself a former Healy Stooge, remembers Moe as quiet and serious. "I was close with the other guys," says Garner, "but I never could get close to Moe."

Emil Sitka recalls that on the set Moe insisted on having the last word on how a scene was to be played. "Moe would listen to my suggestions, and a lot of times he wouldn't agree, but that was the way we did the scene sometimes," says Sitka.

Larry Fine, on the other hand, paid little attention to the filming at hand. "He was more interested in the ball game and placing bets on horses than doing the scene," says Sitka. "He couldn't wait to get the scene over with. As soon as we would finish, Larry would run over to somebody on the set and ask how the Dodgers were doing. Moe would be discussing the scene with the director, but Larry was usually off somewhere else."

"Larry was happy-go-lucky," says Babe Howard, Shemp's widow. "He couldn't have cared less about the act."

For this reason, Moe often domineered Larry offscreen as well as in the act. When Larry made occasional suggestions on the set or during story conferences, they usually had little to do with the story at hand, and he received verbal abuse from Moe as a result.

"Larry's ideas were generally wild and offbeat," says Ed Bernds. "Moe would speak roughly to him, and complain about his suggestions. But once in a while, Larry would come up with an idea that was wild, but a good one, and we would be able to use it."

According to Emil Sitka, Larry seldom "walked through" a scene to acquaint himself with the peculiarities of the set. His partners, on the other hand, usually thoroughly examined every prop they would use during shooting, thus decreasing the possibility of error. Larry, however, would occasionally make mistakes due to his lack of preparation. "He might try to open a door the wrong way," says Sitka, "and that would ruin the scene."

Sitka adds that Moe usually responded to Larry's mistakes by assaulting him with some sort of acid-tongued remark.

"Larry," says Sitka, "was probably the least conscientious of the Stooges."

But Larry has been described as a warm, likeable human being. "Larry was a quiet guy—he didn't talk much," says Mousie Garner, who met Larry during their Healy days. "But he was a very nice guy, and we became good friends."

Curly Howard, in turn, was a warm and friendly person and a genuine extrovert. By all accounts, Curly's personality was the antithesis of Moe's.

Babe Howard said Curly was a generous man. "He'd give you the shirt off his back," she says.

"Curly was a pretty fun-loving guy," says Mousie Garner. "He drank a lot, and he threw his money away; he loved to have a good time. And he was quite a talker. He was really a fun guy to be around—just the opposite of the other two."

Curly did quite well for himself in real estate, investing much of his stage and studio salaries in land purchases.

Unfortunately, Curly's life took a tragic turn in the mid-1940s. After his initial stroke, Curly reportedly underwent what might be described as a personality change.

"When I first met Curly he was no longer a

Curly Howard, age twenty,
with a full head of hair.

The original Three Stooges? Moe and Shemp pose with an unidentified performer in 1917.

19

Curly and Shemp Howard pose with their father, Solomon Horwitz.

well man," says Emil Sitka, "and he was a really serious guy. When I was introduced to him, he actually called me 'sir,' as if I was somebody with dignity!"

It became evident from his movie appearances that Curly had lost much of his characteristic mirth and comic spirit; after his illness, he became a quiet, serious man, much like his two partners.

"Too much sex, too much drinking—that's what ruined Curly," says Babe Howard.

Curly had a series of unsuccessful marriages; he married his last wife, Valerie, after he became ill. She stayed by his side as he spent the last years of his life in a rest home. After enduring a series of strokes, Curly died in 1952.

Curly, as well as his partners, lived in North Hollywood, minutes from Columbia's studio in downtown Hollywood.

Although Curly is generally regarded as the "funniest" member of the team, most of the people who knew and worked with the Three Stooges contend that his brother, Shemp Howard, was actually the most "naturally funny" member of the group. He has also been characterized as the gentlest and most sensitive of the Stooges. Ed Bernds says that beneath his gruff exterior, Shemp was basically a shy person.

"He looked and sounded tough," says Bernds, "but he was really a pretty gentle, easygoing guy."

"Shemp loved to laugh, and he loved to make other people laugh, too," says Babe Howard.

According to Emil Sitka, while Moe would discuss a forthcoming scene, Shemp would keep his ideas to himself. "He'd be listening, and he seldom had anything to say in discussing a scene, but, by God, when the cameras started rolling and the action started, he did his thing, and more so!" says Sitka. "Because his ad libs were good. Shemp knew his business, but he didn't add anything. Shemp was a real pro within his own role."

"Shemp was the funniest of the Stooges," says Mousie Garner, "and the nicest, too."

Shemp and his wife Babe also lived in North Hollywood until Shemp's death in 1955.

Shemp's replacement, Joe Besser, was a relative latecomer to the act. Jules White, who produced and directed all of the Stooges comedies featuring Besser, has said that Besser was a cooperative performer, and he enjoyed working with him as one of the Stooges.

Besser himself found the experiences rewarding. "I enjoyed every minute of it," says Besser. "It was a lot of fun working with the Stooges."

Besser has often cited his "one inspiration" in show business as being children. "I've always had fun with the kids," he says. "They've been good to me, and I've always enjoyed them. It's kind of a mutual thing."

Besser still receives correspondence from fans, complimenting him on his work with and without the Stooges. "My fans know more about me than I know about myself," he says. "They remind me of things I did that I don't even remember doing."

Besser lives in the North Hollywood area with his wife Ernie. He is semi-retired, although he occasionally supplies character voices for television cartoon programs.

Joe DeRita, in turn, has been described as an experienced performer who garnered a lot of respect from his partners.

"Joe was never the trouper that Shemp was, or even that Curly was," says Ed Bernds. "Joe was kind of touchy, and Moe was very considerate of his feelings. Moe could be very rough on Larry, calling him a 'stupid jerk' and telling him what to do with his 'stupid ideas.' But he was very considerate of Joe. That is, he didn't antagonize him."

Even though he was billed as "Curly Joe," DeRita never attempted to imitate his popular predecessor, Curly Howard. "My size and stature were similar to his," says DeRita, "but I did what I knew was right."

DeRita, who currently resides in North Hollywood with his wife Jean, has also retired from active performing.

All of the various Stooges enjoyed ad libbing, and they were often allowed to improvise at will. Emil Sitka, who began working with the Stooges after Curly's stroke, says Curly, between takes, was very subdued and quiet on the set. "But when the director yelled 'action,' he just turned on."

Jules White says he often had trouble directing the Stooges comedies because of Curly Howard's ad libbing. Curly was so funny that crew members would often break up with laughter, ruining the scene.

"Curly was an artist," declares White. "He invariably could get you a laugh with a nonsensical gesture or something of that sort."

White admits that Curly was his favorite of all the various Stooges. "Curly was outstanding," says White. "Shemp, his brother, who replaced him when the poor boy had a stroke, was also very, very good—but not quite Curly. And Joe Besser was a very cute man in his own way. But I would say that Curly was my favorite Stooge of the Stooges."

Like Curly, Shemp Howard seldom ad libbed during rehearsals, saving his improvisations for the actual take. "Shemp was allowed to ad lib," says Emil Sitka, "especially on a scene that ends. And he came up with some good ones. He'd be the one that we'd laugh at, mostly, on the set."

Joe Besser also ad libbed frequently in his ap-

Shemp and a friend clown with Moe in this snapshot from the 1920s.

Shemp and Babe Howard, newlyweds, in 1925.

Shemp models his wife's coat.

Moe and Shemp, out of costume but still in character.

pearances with the Stooges. Indeed, Besser's improvisations often "saved" a particular scene that would otherwise have fallen flat. Although Besser's character often did not mesh with the personalities of his partners, it frequently was his enthusiasm that "carried" the comedy.

Joe DeRita, as well, brought his own style of comedy to the act. Even though he represented the "Curly" figure of the trio, he played the role in much the same way as he had before teaming with the Stooges. His ad libs were in keeping with his own comic personality.

"Joe DeRita was a comedian in his own right before he became a Stooge," says Emil Sitka, "so he still had his notions as to the way he wanted to do his part. You'll notice he played it differently; he didn't try to be like the original Curly. If I was a director I'd have a hard time telling him what to do. I'd just have to let him do it!"

The Stooges' on-the-set behavior was characterized by their almost constant arguing among themselves.

"The arguments between them were fun," says Sitka, "but you'd have to know the Stooges to appreciate them. They'd argue about the goofiest little thing. That's what was funny about them. They'd argue about things that most people would overlook, like a missing button or a tear in a sleeve."

Sitka recalls an incident on the set that proved to be rather embarrassing for the Stooges. "If a scene didn't go exactly right," says Sitka, "they'd have an argument. And I mean the language was pretty blue! They'd say things like, 'What's the matter with you, you dumb sonofabitch,' and so forth. One time they were going at it, and the lights came on, which meant the end of a scene. And guess what! A group of little kids were being led on the set by their teacher. If you think the Stooges' language didn't change but quick!"

Ed Bernds says the Stooges had a distinct fondness for blue humor, "Some of the anecdotes they told were pretty salty."

They also enjoyed occasional practical jokes. Many of their supporting players at Columbia Pictures were the hapless victims of their prankery.

Actress Lorna Gray, for example, found herself at their mercy during the filming of a comedy in 1940. According to Ed Bernds, a live bear was brought on the set for a scene with the Stooges. Even though it was drugged into harmlessness, Miss Gray was terrified of the animal. Larry Fine took advantage of her fear for a prank. When Lorna wasn't looking, Larry got on his hands and knees, grabbed her by the leg, and let loose a bear

growl. Lorna was so frightened she fainted, and production had to be halted temporarily.

Despite the fact that the Stooges often delighted in scaring their co-workers with such antics, they themselves were often uneasy around animals.

Emil Sitka recalls that during the filming of a comedy featuring Shemp Howard, the boys were quite wary of a live lion used in several scenes with them. But while all of the Stooges were uncomfortable around the animal, Shemp was deathly afraid of the beast.

"Shemp wouldn't work if the lion was in the same scene," says Sitka. "And the lion was sickly-looking. It had flies buzzing around its head. But the propmen put a big plate of glass between the Stooges and the lion when they were filming. And when they finished shooting, Shemp wanted to be a mile away from it."

While relaxing between scenes, however, Shemp discovered that he wasn't quite as far away from the lion as he had thought. When the animal's trainer came looking for the lion to shoot another scene, he found it curled up asleep on the floor directly behind where Shemp was sitting.

The Stooges, according to Ed Bernds, were often not the rough-and-tumble comedians they appeared to be. He describes them as cooperative, but adds there were times when they were afraid of performing certain physical stunts.

Emil Sitka has similar memories of working with the Stooges.

"I was amazed at the things they were afraid of doing," says Sitka.

Despite this, all of the Stooges have been described as basically hard-working performers. They were anything-for-a-laugh comedians who kept America entertained through a nationwide depression and a world war. And today, while our collective economic problems seem worse than ever, and our national security is constantly being challenged, the Three Stooges have reached a new peak of popularity. In the year of their Golden Anniversary, the Stooges have quite possibly become the most popular comedy team in America. Perhaps audiences need their simplistic slapstick antics now more than ever before.

While the theory that the Three Stooges were "masters of comedy" may be a little overblown, they were, in fact, seasoned professionals who knew their craft and knew it well.

And after half a century, the Three Stooges have become, in every sense of the phrase, "a legend of comedy."

Early portrait of Ted Healy, the man who assembled what later became the Three Stooges.

Emergence of a Team

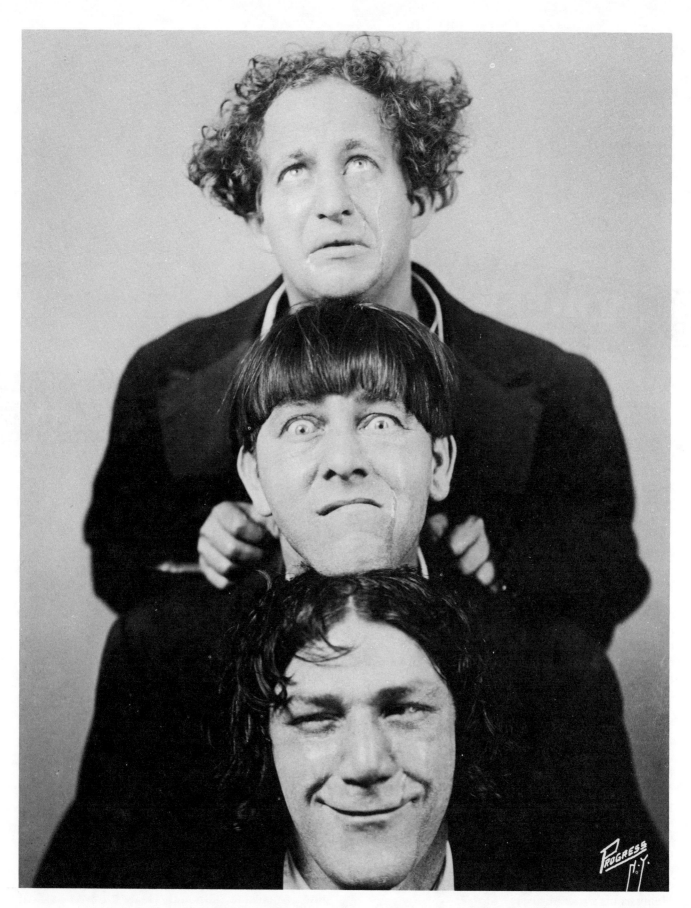

Larry Fine (top) joins Moe and Shemp Howard as Stooges in 1925.

Chapter Two

It is safe to assume that the "Three Stooges" would never have come into being if it had not been for Ted Healy. Healy was a brilliant comedian, and through his guidance the Stooges rose to success in show business. Although some of the Stooges have indicated that Healy used them to further his own career, Healy's influence on the Stooges and their style of comedy extended to every aspect of their act. Years after they went out on their own—years after Healy's death—the Stooges still used vaudeville material they had performed with Healy during their early years as a team.

This chapter, therefore, should not be considered part of the history of the "Three Stooges," per se, but rather a study of how the Stooges came together, how their characters and comic routines evolved, and how one man formed what was to become one of the most popular comedy acts of all time.

Today, Ted Healy has been all but forgotten. Most references to Healy say little more than the fact that he brought the Three Stooges to Hollywood. This is a shame, because during his day Healy was one of the top comedians in the business. By the late 1920s, Healy was one of the most popular performers in vaudeville. He established himself as a great improvisational comic, and his style and mannerisms were quickly imitated by dozens of vaudeville gagsters. Milton Berle, for example, is among the many comedians who patterned himself after Healy. Even today, Berle cites Healy as his show business "idol."

Healy's physical appearance was a significant part of his comedy. While he wasn't a buffoon character in the sense that his Stooges were, he nevertheless strived for a comic appearance. Always attired in a cheap suit and hat, he often carried a cigar or cigarette as well. Healy's facial expression was one of sour cynicism, a reflection of his acerbic comic personality. But perhaps the most memorable aspect of Healy's stage character was his walk. With arms swinging confidently at his sides, Healy walked briskly, chest out, giving him an air of assertiveness.

Throughout his career, Healy had a dozen or more different Stooges. Some of them branched out to form independent acts of their own; the "Three Stooges" are among them.

The Three Stooges developed into recognizable comic characters once they left Healy to pursue a career on their own. During their Healy days, however, they played little more than mute observers of Healy's antics.

A newspaper interview with Eddie Moran, himself a Healy Stooge in the 1930s, reveals the secret of becoming an effective Healy second. "A stooge must never act," said Moran. "He must be himself even to the point of recognizing friends and waving to them." Moran also pointed out that "blank naturalness" was the "most essential part of the art of stooging."

The Three Stooges established characters for themselves, however, shortly after leaving Healy: Moe was the antagonist figure; Larry, the hapless middleman; and Curly, the patsy of the group. But during their tenure with Healy they were basically interchangeable, although Healy allowed each of them to exploit occasionally their individual talents.

Moe's position as ''boss'' of the team seems to have been taken over by someone else in this family snapshot.

Shemp poses with a pair of locals while on tour with the Stooges in the late '20s.

Healy's first threesome was assembled in the early 1920s. Healy's original Stooges consisted of three comics, Lou Warren, Dick Hakins, and Shemp Howard. All three of these men eventually left Healy to pursue independent careers on their own.

Lou Warren left Healy's entourage in 1925, never to return to the act. Dick Hakins left shortly afterward due to illness, but returned several years later with two other "Stooges." And Shemp Howard eventually brought in his brother Moe Howard, and later Larry Fine, thus completing Healy's second Stooges ensemble. Healy had grown up with the Howard brothers, and had met Larry Fine in vaudeville. It is this trio that is generally regarded as the "original" Healy Stooges, although research has shown this to be false.

Despite frequent personnel changes in Healy's act, all of his "Stooges" were "stooges" both onstage and off. In addition to playing second bananas to Healy in his vaudeville act, they were often required to socialize with him as well. Healy brought his Stooges with him practically everywhere; he seemed to have an obsession about having his men around him constantly.

One story cited by Mousie Garner, who became a Stooge in the 1930s, exemplifies the extent of Healy's obsession. While Healy and the Stooges were appearing on Broadway during the Depression, Healy had become quite popular with Manhattan's elite society. A wealthy socialite fell in love with Healy, and he soon found himself living with her in her Madison Avenue home. One day, Healy invited his Stooges over to her home for a visit. When they arrived, Healy was in bed with the woman. Without so much as a blink, Healy told his Stooges to hop into bed with him!

Healy has also been described as incredibly generous. "He was the most generous man I ever came in contact with," says Mousie Garner. "He always made money, but he never had any because he gave it all away! He was so wrapped up in helping people; his only love in life was helping people out."

Garner remembers one instance in which Healy was unable to pay his Stooges their weekly salary. Healy took them aside, and asked them, "Wouldn't you rather have two hundred dollars next week, instead of only a hundred dollars this week?" The Stooges agreed, and Healy paid them in full the following week, throwing in a box of expensive cigars as interest.

Aside from his personal eccentricities, Healy was one of the most innovative performers vaudeville ever produced. "He was even crazier offstage than he was on," professes Mousie Garner.

Healy's personality has been described as magnetic, and perhaps this is one of the reasons why his Stooges put up with his often erratic behavior. An original "nut" comic, Healy created and developed the concept of using "stooges," and was literally the first comedian in vaudeville to actually slap his partners in the face.

"Healy started the business of slapping in comedy," says Mousie Garner. "Other comedians had pretended to hit each other before, but Healy was the first guy who actually *did* it."

But despite the "realism" of Healy's comedy, little pain was ever suffered by his Stooges. Dick Hakins remembers barely feeling Healy's facial slaps. "He was a big man, and he had big hands," says Hakins, "but his palms were so soft you never even felt it."

The group that later evolved into the "Three Stooges" was assembled in 1925. Healy had hired Shemp Howard, and Shemp's brother Moe, as his comic foils. Shortly afterward, musician Larry Fine became a member of the trio. While Healy and the Stooges were playing Chicago, they caught the stage show at a local night club. Among the performers was a tuxedoed entertainer who did a Russian dance while playing the violin. Healy and the Stooges were impressed with the young man's comic appearance, and he was offered the position of a Stooge at a hundred dollars a week. Thus, Larry Fine threw away his fiddle and became the middleman of the act in 1925.

As the 1920s progressed, so did the popularity of Healy and the Stooges. By the end of the decade, they were appearing in lavish comedy revues on Broadway, performing basically the same kind of material they had used in vaudeville. One routine had Healy hanging from a chin-up bar high above the stage while the Stooges supported him with a ladder from below. They would keep taking the ladder away, causing Healy to scream for help. The boys would stumble back and forth, knocking down scenery and backdrops. This routine was reworked by the Stooges when they went out on their own, with Moe taking Healy's place on the ladder and his partners dragging it out from under him. In fact, most of the routines and sketches the Stooges performed with Healy were eventually reworked for their own act.

After a year of top vaudeville bookings throughout the country in 1928, Healy and the Stooges opened on Broadway in "A Night in Venice" (1929), featuring musical numbers staged by Busby Berkely. A number of routines from the show were reused by the Three Stooges throughout their career.

When "A Night in Venice" was closed by the Depression in 1930, Healy and his partners re-

Three of Healy's Stooges from the 1930s: from left, Dick Hakins, Mousie Garner and Sammy Wolf. This trio also worked under the name "Gentlemaniacs."

turned to vaudeville, using many of their routines from the revue. That same year Healy and the Stooges acquired a booking at New York's famed Palace Theater, then the most prestigious vaudeville house in the country. A talent scout from Hollywood's Fox Studios, the forerunner of 20th Century-Fox, caught their act and signed Healy and the Stooges for a feature film appearance. SOUP TO NUTS (1930), written by Rube Goldberg, marked the screen debut of the Stooges.

The plotline of SOUP TO NUTS simply served as a backdrop for the standard vaudeville routines of Healy and the Stooges. Leonard Maltin has noted that the Stooges appeared in the film as firemen who assist Healy in breaking up a party.

While the Stooges' screen time was minimal (they didn't even receive billing), SOUP TO NUTS is significant in that the Stooges were offered a separate film contract as a result of their appearance. Thus, the Stooges made arrangements to leave their mentor and sign with Fox as a trio. Healy interfered, however, and Fox called the deal off.

Angry with Healy, the Stooges decided to go out on their own anyway. Jack Walsh, a straight man, was hired to replace Healy, and the Stooges began developing material of their own. The trio continued working without their mentor for a couple of years, building a reputation of their own as a starring act rather than as a group of second bananas.

During this period both Healy and his former Stooges were using much of the same material. Shemp Howard, however, created a new addition to the Stooges' act, although in a rather unorthodox manner.

According to Babe Howard, the addition came about one afternoon as the Stooges and their wives were relaxing between stage shows. "We were all sitting around playing cards, and passing time," says Babe. "Shemp had a terrible temper, and he thought Larry was cheating. So he jumped up and yelled, 'I'm gonna stab your eyes out!' He actually poked Larry right in the eyes with his fingers! Moe, who was the brains of the outfit, always had a sharp eye for something new for the act. So he decided to include that bit in their routines."

By now Moe Howard had established himself as the boss and businessman of the trio. He became the driving force of the Stooges, securing performing dates and contracts for the act as well as devising many of their routines and sketches.

As the Stooges were establishing themselves, Healy, in turn, hired three other "second bananas" to replace them in his act. These Stooges had already had extensive vaudeville experience prior to teaming with Healy; each of them was a

The boys with a couple of visitors during a vaudeville engagement in the 1930s.

musician and a comedian, and each had been a professional performer for years before becoming members of the second Stooges trio.

Jack Wolf was the antagonist figure of the new group; he played the character that dished out all the slapping and eye-poking to his partners. Wolf was an astute businessman, and he later arranged performing contracts and vaudeville engagements for the team. He was also a talented musician, and his musical abilities were often showcased in appearances with the Stooges.

Dick Hakins returned to play the "middleman" of the threesome. He had started out in show business as a musician, and had scored several Broadway shows prior to working for Healy. Hakins was brought back into the act primarily because of his dry sense of humor and ability to look sappy when necessary.

Mousie Garner, the new "Third Stooge," played the patsy figure of the act. Garner was Jack

31

Wolf's cousin, and they had broken into show business together as a comedy act prior to teaming with Dick Hakins as Healy's Stooges. Like his partners, Garner was also a musician, and his comic piano playing routine became a staple of the act.

All three of Healy's new Stooges had met prior to joining Healy, having previously appeared in vaudeville together. But it was Healy who first hired them as a team, and it wasn't until they appeared with Healy that they were called "Stooges." In fact, they were the first comics actually billed as Healy's Stooges; prior to that, Healy's Stooges had been called everything from "Mr. Healy's Men" to "Southern Gentlemen."

All three "new" men were serious musicians, even though they played primarily for laughs when appearing as Stooges. One routine had all three Stooges playing one piano at the same time. In addition to playing instruments, Healy's new trio sang and danced. They introduced the popular Depression-era hit "Million Dollar Baby," which they performed in one of their musical revues.

"Our act was like the Three Stooges with music," says Mousie Garner. "We did the same kind of physical comedy as the Stooges, but we could also play instruments and sing."

Dick Hakins points out that their act wasn't as violent as that of the Three Stooges, even though they indulged in a lot of physical mayhem themselves. Newspaper reviews of both Stooges acts from the 1930s indicate that the content of both trios was somewhat similar. In addition, Healy's "new" threesome also sported gag haircuts and wore similar stage costumes. And, of course, they were also fairly short in stature, as were the original members. None of the various Stooges stood more than five-and-a-half feet tall.

After a couple of years of performing with his new threesome, Healy was forced to take a substantial salary cut due to the Depression. As a result, he had to drop his second set of Stooges. They, in turn, went out on their own (not as "Stooges," but as "Gentlemaniacs"), and departed for performing engagements in Great Britain. Healy's second ensemble spent several months overseas, headlining the London Palladium as well as theaters throughout the continent.

Healy's new Stooges had developed an act that was similar in many ways to the "Three Stooges," but distinctly different in style. There was less emphasis on violence, even though they employed such traditional bits as the "poke in the eyes." One bit they used quite frequently was nicknamed the "mob scene." This consisted of the boys milling around in circles around each other, creating the effect of crowding and confusion!

Healy was replaced in their act, more or less, by a straight man, who introduced the trio and reacted to their antics. His name was Jack Walsh —the same straight man Healy's other trio had used several years earlier.

After Healy's death years later, his second set of Stooges decided to capitalize on the association with him. They also began billing themselves as the "Three Stooges," and made a number of appearances under that name. They even had their own series of movie comedies in the 1930s, several years before the "original" Three Stooges signed with Columbia.

Healy's second "Three Stooges" headlined the vaudeville circuit both here and abroad, and they frequently crossed paths with the "other" Three Stooges. *Variety* reported that the "original" Stooges had planned to take the other trio to court, in an attempt to stop them from using their name in their billing. Mousie Garner, however, has denied that the case ever got that far.

"If anything," says Garner, "the publicity would have helped us."

Healy's second group eventually gave in, however, and stopped using the "Three Stooges" name.

While both sets of Stooges were establishing themselves in the early 1930s, Healy received a raise in salary, and was again in a position to rehire his Stooges. He had contacted his former Stooges working in Europe, but they had a number of contractual obligations to fulfill and were unable to rejoin him. Then, Healy attempted to rehire his other ensemble. He was successful, and, after months of deliberation, they returned to his act.

Strange as it may seem, all of Healy's various Stooges were friends. They often socialized together. They had become acquainted with each other during their vaudeville days through their mutual association with Healy. If Shemp Howard was temporarily unavailable to play the "Third Stooge," for example, Healy might ask Mousie Garner to leave his own act and take his place. As members of Healy's entourage they were virtually interchangeable, because they had not yet identified themselves with audiences as definite characters.

"But Healy really preferred working with Moe and Shemp," says Babe Howard. "They had grown up with him, and he knew Larry very well, too. He knew the way they ad libbed."

Despite their friendship with him, Healy delighted in tormenting his Stooges, usually while under the influence of alcohol. "Healy was a conniver," points out Babe Howard, "and he had a mean sense of humor. He'd do terrible things to

Shemp Howard, solo comedian, as he appeared while under contract at Universal Pictures,
after leaving the Stooges.

the boys, especially Shemp, just to see the terrified look on his face.''

Reportedly Healy had a habit of inviting his Stooges over to his house as overnight guests. But when he started drinking, the Stooges quickly packed their suitcases and headed out of the building. Experience had taught them that that was the best thing to do. Because Healy, while drunk, would become angry and belligerent. He would take all of their clothes and personal belongings, and simply toss them out the windows, for no apparent reason other than to irritate the Stooges.

Healy also enjoyed pulling elaborate practical jokes on the Stooges, and, often, innocent bystanders. While living in a Hollywood hotel in the 1930s, Healy once instructed his Stooges to gather up about a hundred telephone directories. When they did so, they brought them up to Healy's penthouse suite. Healy got quite a kick out of dropping them out the window, trying to hit people on the street below.

Dick Hakins remembers a story told to him by Healy about his original Stooges ensemble. ''Healy brought all three of them to a Catholic church,'' says Hakins. ''Healy was Catholic, but the Stooges were Jewish. They asked Healy to show them what to do. He just told them to do whatever he did. So they all went up to the front pew, and sat down. Every time the priest turned around, Healy would stand up, or sit down, or kneel, just to watch the poor guys jumping up and down in confusion! Afterwards, Shemp told him he'd never go to a church again—too much jumping up and down!''

When it came to returning to work with Healy as Stooges, Shemp Howard, however, was no longer interested. ''I was really the one that made Shemp go out on his own,'' says Babe Howard. ''I was sick and tired of Healy, and of all of his tricks, so I told Shemp to take a movie offer he had gotten.''

Shemp did, and began work as a solo comedian at Vitagraph Studios. He appeared in a number of two-reel comedies over a period of several years.

Healy, however, was less than pleased when his star ''Stooge'' left the act. Shemp had suggested that they use his younger brother, Jerry Howard, as a replacement, but Healy wasn't interested. Not only was Healy unimpressed with the idea, but the other Stooges were, too.

''Moe wrote Shemp a letter,'' says Babe Howard, ''telling him that Jerry had absolutely no talent. Moe did not want him in the act. Jerry didn't have a lot of experience in show business, but he wanted to get in, even if Moe didn't want him.''

So Shemp devised a scheme to get Jerry into the act. He told him to shave his head and run on stage barefoot! Jerry did so, and, because of his haircut, acquired the name ''Curly'' as well. As a result of his rather grotesque appearance, Curly got a tremendous laugh from the audience. That was enough to convince all concerned that Curly was a suitable replacement for Shemp.

Curly eventually developed his own unique comic style, creating a character whose actions and personality suggested a blend of insanity and childlike ignorance. With his shaven head, rotund appearance and use of comic high-pitched voice, Curly resembled, as Moe put it, ''a fat fairy.''

''Curly was never really an actor,'' says Babe Howard. ''He was really imitating Hugh Herbert.'' But it was Curly who clicked with the Stooges, and he quickly became the star of the trio, outshining his partners as well as his predecessor.

''After Shemp quit,'' says Babe Howard, ''Curly became the funniest Stooge.''

Healy and the Stooges went back into vaudeville in 1932, and Curly quickly adapted to the style of the act. While making an appearance at a Hollywood night club that same year, Healy and his partners were enlisted by an agent from MGM Studios to perform at a charity benefit.

Following their performance, MGM signed Healy and the Stooges to a one-year contract at that prestigious studio. While at MGM, Healy and the Stooges appeared in several feature films and a number of two-reel comedies, some filmed in color. The bulk of these were musical efforts, and Healy generally received more attention than his three Stooges.

But even though the Stooges were working steadily in both vaudeville and movies, it was becoming clear that their development as a team was being hampered by their second banana status. It was not until the Stooges decided to go out on their own on a permanent basis that they were able to fully develop their madcap style of comedy.

During their year at MGM, Healy and the Stooges were used both separately and together as a team in features and shorts. Healy was especially prolific as a single, appearing in a number of features with some of MGM's biggest stars. The Stooges, meanwhile, did occasional work without their mentor as well. Before long, both Healy and the Stooges realized they would be better off as separate acts. Thus, in early 1934, an amicable legal agreement was drawn up, stating that Healy and the Stooges would no longer be considered a team.

Moe Howard, Larry Fine and Curly Howard

Men of distinction: Curly Howard joins brother Moe and Larry Fine in the 1930s.

decided to try to make it on their own as a trio, leaving Healy for good to pursue an independent career. Healy, in turn, granted them permission to use the name "Three Stooges." Shortly after the Stooges left MGM, they were picked up by Columbia Pictures to star in two-reel comedies. Jules White, formerly a producer and director at MGM, had just been put in charge of developing Columbia's two-reel comedy department. He had known the Stooges when they were part of Healy's act, and hired them immediately for Columbia.

Healy, however, continued to make appearances with other Stooges. To replace his departing trio, Healy rehired his other set of Stooges from several years earlier. They had returned from their European tour and were working at home at the time. Healy wired them and asked them to return to his act as his "Super Stooges."

But Jack Wolf had already retired from performing and a replacement was needed. Wolf was replaced in the act by Sammy Glaser, another friend of Healy's, who was renamed "Sammy Wolf." A contract for the "Super Stooges" was drawn up at MGM, even though they never actually appeared in a film as Healy's "Stooges." Most of the work they did during this period was in stage and radio appearances with Healy in the Hollywood area.

"I told Healy it was too late to start another Stooges act," says Mousie Garner. "I said the Three Stooges had made it big on their own, and we'd missed the boat! But he insisted we get back together with him."

Garner contends that Healy was well on his way to bigger and better things when he rehired his replacement Stooges ensemble. "Warner Brothers had Healy on loan-out from MGM," says Garner, "and they wanted to make a big star out of him. He had done a picture called VARSITY SHOW, and then HOLLYWOOD HOTEL, for them. And he stole both pictures, even without Stooges. As Stooges, we were in on the filming of HOLLY-WOOD HOTEL, but we never turned up in the final print. Actually, we had nothing to do with the plot. Absolutely nothing! Healy had signed us to a contract for the film while he was drinking!"

Oddly enough, VARSITY SHOW (1937), in which Healy appears as a solo performer, has a character referring to Healy as "stooge!" It turned out to be one of his last movie appearances; he died shortly after the film's release.

In 1937, while celebrating the birth of Ted Junior, his first child at a nightclub on Sunset Boulevard in Hollywood, Healy got into an argument with two other patrons. He threatened to take them outside and beat both of them up, one at a time. Healy's drinking had always made him belligerent, and this was ultimately his downfall. Had his Stooges been with him, Healy probably would never have gotten into the argument in the first place.

"But nobody would drink with him," says Mousie Garner, "because he became a different person when he was drunk."

"He always got pugilistic when he was drinking," adds Dick Hakins. "But he couldn't fight, and that's why he got killed."

Reportedly, when Healy stepped outside the club for the fight, both men jumped him and beat him severely, leaving him bleeding on the sidewalk. Healy suffered a brain concussion, and died shortly afterward. At the time of his death, Healy was one of the biggest comedians in vaudeville, earning one of the largest salaries in the business.

Healy's untimely death left all of his Stooges in a state of shock. Healy's "Super Stooges" served as pallbearers at his funeral in Culver City. All of Healy's Stooges were in attendance, even though Shemp Howard hated funerals.

"Shemp was so nervous he brought along a tiny flask of whiskey to calm his nerves," says Mousie Garner. "He would take a nip at it every once in a while. And Shemp didn't even drink, to speak of. He was really uncomfortable."

With the death of Ted Healy, show business lost one of its greatest performers. It seems a shame that one of vaudeville's finest comedians is today virtually forgotten, remembered only in references to the comedy team that he created.

Prime Years of Popularity

To My
Brother"
Shemp
From Your
Loveing
Brother
"Babe"

Nov. 16. 1933

Curly Howard, also nicknamed "Babe," the most popular of the various Stooges.

Chapter Three

The Columbia "shorts department" was a hectic place in the 1930s. A separate entity from the company's feature film division, the department occupied a building on Beechwood Drive in Hollywood, across the street from Columbia's main studio. The close-knit shorts department had its own sound stages, its own producers and directors, and its own stars.

Of the three critically acknowledged "geniuses" of silent comedy, Charlie Chaplin, Buster Keaton and Harry Langdon, only Chaplin managed to avoid the Columbia two-reelers. The Columbia shorts were generally considered the bottom of the barrel in terms of artistic quality, as well as financial reward for the performers who appeared in them. Chaplin had amassed enormous wealth and was able to turn out his own silent films long after talkies had established themselves. But within a few years after the advent of movie sound, both Keaton and Langdon found themselves broke. Both of them were forced to turn out shorts at Columbia, for considerably less money than they had earned during their silent-era heyday.

Columbia became a haven for has-been comedians. In addition to former stars from the silent era, future stars began their movie careers at Columbia as well. Lucille Ball, Lloyd Bridges and others popped up in early Three Stooges shorts. Stars were constantly coming and going at Columbia, finding short-term work in two-reelers between feature film assignments at Columbia and other studios.

These shorts, each less than twenty minutes in length, were produced by the studio as "curtain raisers" to be shown before the feature film presentation. Studio management considered the shorts to be "throwaways," and they paid little attention to their production—as long as they were completed on schedule.

Because each short had to be shot in less than a week, time was of the essence. At Columbia most of them had to be filmed in three days. The Stooges, however, were usually allowed an extra day of shooting time, primarily because of the often elaborate sight gags involved. Emil Sitka, who began work at Columbia in the 1940s, reports that sometimes half a day would be spent preparing and filming one single gag.

"I was surprised they shot the entire film in only a few days," he says. "It was a tight schedule, believe me! We really had to squeeze it in. We'd work a full day, and get a good many scenes in the can, but on the last day there was always a rush to get it in before five o'clock."

Indeed, Columbia's comedy factory was among the busiest lots in Hollywood. By the 1940s, Columbia had the largest two-reel comedy unit in operation. The shorts, in turn, were among Columbia's most consistently popular attractions.

But in 1934, not many people would have guessed that the shorts department's newest acquisition, the "Three Stooges," would soon become its most valuable property.

"I had dozens of great comedians," says Jules White, head of Columbia's two-reeler unit. "Some of 'em were world renowned. Buster Keaton was, I daresay, one of the three biggest in the history of comedy. Harry Langdon came much later; he was also a giant. So the Stooges were not the only ones

I made pictures with. But television has boosted them to the sky, and they've overshadowed anything else we've ever done as far as public taste is concerned.''

At the time the Stooges were hired by Columbia, the studio was in the process of developing its two-reel comedy unit and was in search of new talent. Comedy veteran White headed the department during the first several years of its existence. Hugh McCollum, former secretary to Columbia president Harry Cohn, later split production duties with White. White had many years of experience under his belt as both a producer and director. He had worked his way up from gag man and film editor at Educational Pictures to producer and director at MGM. After hiring the Stooges for Columbia, he saw to it that they were supplied with good writers and directors, as well as talented supporting players.

Columbia paid the Stooges a yearly salary totaling $60,000, which was split between them. Even though they started at the figure in 1934, they never received a raise in pay, despite the fact that they were with Columbia for nearly a quarter of a century.

"Columbia made millions off the Stooges," says Edward Bernds, "and they're still making money."

Babe Howard points out the Stooges made most of their money from personal appearances, not through their studio salary. "At Columbia, they worked for peanuts," she says.

In addition, the Stooges never received a dime in residual payments from the Columbia shorts. In the early 1960s, the Screen Actors' Guild, then headed by Ronald Reagan, passed a ruling that no residuals would be paid for films made before 1960. The last Three Stooges short was released in 1959, leaving the Stooges high and dry.

During the Depression, however, $60,000 was an enormous amount of money, and the Stooges were happy to sign with Columbia. They were assured that they would have the best people working with them on their films, many of whom were personal friends of Jules White.

White hired a number of comedy "greats" to work for him, including former partner Del Lord. White and Lord had started out in the business together, working for the Mack Sennett studio during the silent era. According to White, Lord worked as a stunt driver for Sennett, and was eventually promoted to director. By the 1930s, however, the short comedy business was on a definite decline. Del Lord subsequently found himself out of the movies and selling used cars. Upon hearing of this, White hired him immediately.

"He had no business ever getting out of the business," says White, "but he had a funny habit of eating."

Lord turned out to be one of the comedy department's greatest assets; his filmmaking experience and knowledge of physical comedy were invaluable. As a director, Lord even threw his own pies. Mack Sennett himself credited Lord as being the foremost "pie thrower" in the business.

"Del Lord made some terrific films for me," says White. "He was a great gag man, a great story man, and he was good on the stunts because

Shemp Howard and an unidentified studio employee pose with the Stooges on the set of PARDON MY SCOTCH (1935). Shemp was already appearing in his own series of shorts as a solo performer.

he had done them. He was really very valuable to me.''

Most of the Stooges' best work was, in fact, accomplished under Lord's direction, whose sense of timing and flair for comedy was unparalleled. Lord remained at Columbia throughout the 1930s and '40s, working with people like Buster Keaton and Harry Langdon as well as the Stooges. Lord even wrote several Three Stooges scripts, all of which were loaded with familiar gags from his silent comedy days.

Another comedy great who eventually found himself on the Columbia roster and working with the Stooges was Charley Chase. Chase was one of the most versatile people in the business, just as much at home serving as comedian, writer and director. Chase was the star of his own series during the silent era, and he continued to have success when talkies became popular, working in two-reelers at the Hal Roach Studios. Roach and Sennett were the two major movie comedy factories of the 1920s and early '30s. By the late 1930s, however, Roach decided to abandon its shorts department. As a result, Chase was fired from the studio. Jules White grasped this opportunity and Chase, too, was signed with Columbia. Chase directed a number of films with the Stooges, and, like Lord, he lifted many of his favorite gags and routines from his earlier comedies for them.

Another comedy veteran whom White hired was his brother Jack. Jack White, as a teenager, had been a comedy director for Mack Sennett and was head of his own movie company at the age of twenty. White also produced two-reel comedies, all of which were released through Educational Pictures. Following his tenure of work for Educational, Jack White was hired as a writer and director by brother Jules. Jack directed several of the Stooges' earliest comedies under the pseudonym ''Preston Black,'' and later contributed to their film scripts in the 1940s and '50s as Jack White. As a writer, White often missed his mark when working with the Stooges, although several of his directorial efforts are better than average. White continued to work with the Stooges as a writer or director throughout their years of service at Columbia, remaining there until their final year of production.

Columbia quickly established an impressive roster of comedy experts. ''I have a theory,'' Jules White said recently, ''that old talent never dies. It may hide for a while, but it never dies. And all of these men verified that.''

Curiously enough, with all that experience and talent available, the first film the Stooges appeared in at Columbia was WOMAN HATERS (1934), an odd musical comedy with the dialogue spoken completely in rhyme. Even stranger is the fact that the Stooges appear separately, not as a team. Moe and Curly are pushed into the background, while Larry receives a lot of screen time as a member of the Woman Haters Club who secretly gets married. Although the film is supplied with a fine cast of supporting actors, many of them talented comedians in their own right, the short itself is a rather weak effort. WOMAN HATERS suffers from gratuitous physical violence, apparently in an attempt to capitalize on what the Stooges were becoming famous for.

Their second Columbia comedy, PUNCH DRUNKS (1934), is a vast improvement over their initial effort. Again the Stooges appear as separate characters, but in a situation related to their comic personalities. The story, written by the Stooges themselves, has Curly as a waiter who goes berserk whenever he hears ''Pop Goes the Weasel.'' Moe plays a fight manager who wants to make Curly the new champ, and Larry portrays a wandering musician hired to provide the music that drives Curly crazy. The plot is decidedly absurd, but the Stooges' personalities keep the film moving at a fast pace.

Their third Columbia short, MEN IN BLACK (1934), was nominated for an Academy Award. It is difficult today to imagine why that particular film was chosen as a contender for an Oscar; the short is virtually plotless and the wild sight gags are silly, rather than funny. The somewhat incongruous script was written by Felix Adler, who served as a writer for the Stooges until the end of their Columbia career more than twenty years later. Adler was a vastly experienced gagman, and by the end of his career, he had written for nearly every major slapstick comedian in show business.

Columbia forced the Stooges to experiment with various directors in the early 1930s; writers like Lou Breslow and Clyde Bruckman even tried their hand at directing, with pleasing results. Bruckman in particular was rated an excellent director, although he was considered primarily a writer. He had served as Buster Keaton's head gag writer and later wrote for Harold Lloyd. Bruckman wrote some of the Stooges' best scripts, with ingenious sight gags and clever gag situations. Like Felix Adler, Bruckman had hundreds of movie credits under his belt, and he worked with nearly every great slapstick comic in Hollywood until his tragic suicide in the 1950s.

Jules White recently reflected upon the aggregate talent of the Columbia two-reeler writing staff. ''These men were infallible,'' he said. ''You could say, 'I want this and this and this, see what you can do with it, see what you can concoct,' and

Del Lord, the man who helped establish the Three Stooges as a comedy team after they left their mentor.

you could bet your red apples out of a barrel of rotten ones they'd come up with something good.''

White adds there was much discussion of the rough script between the writer and director before the finished product was completed. "We'd work and interchange ideas, and come up with a two-reel comedy," he explains.

Despite the highly-qualified writers and directors available to them, the Stooges, during their early years at Columbia, faced a major problem defining their screen characters. In vaudeville, it was not necessary for the Stooges to portray reasonably believable personalities; in films, however, it was. When they started work at Columbia, they had not yet established definite comic characters for themselves, and many misfire gags resulted from this. For instance, in MEN IN BLACK, Larry slaps Moe, but Moe doesn't do anything to Larry in return. This bit would be almost unheard of in any of the later Stooges comedies, yet this kind of gag occasionally popped up in their early shorts.

This situation was quickly remedied when Del Lord began work with them. He helped them develop their screen characters into somewhat believable personalities, raising their status from absurd ruffians without characterization to believable, yet farcical, comic performers.

Lord's first Stooges comedy, POP GOES THE EASEL (1935) is highlighted by a hilarious clay-throwing melee in an art school. EASEL deftly blends the vaudeville-style antics of the Stooges with the broad visual humor and sight gags of silent comedy. In these early efforts with Lord, the Stooges performed with energy and enthusiasm that was often missing from their later films. While the actual scripts of shorts like POP GOES THE EASEL were often rather flimsy, the masterful direction of Lord and the performances of the Stooges brought the shorts to a respectable level of comic quality.

PARDON MY SCOTCH (1935), another early comedy directed by Lord, is highlighted by a sequence in which the Stooges are seen as carpenters. One of the most breathtaking stunts ever performed in a Stooges comedy has Moe standing on a table while Curly cuts down the middle of it with a power saw. When Moe turns to his partners, the table collapses and Moe crashes to the floor. The effect is hilarious, but Moe actually broke several ribs in the fall. After speaking several words, Moe fainted and was hospitalized for several days. The scene was considered so good that it was later spliced into another Stooges comedy, DIZZY DETECTIVES (1943), directed by Jules white.

The best of Lord's early shorts with the Stooges is HOI POLLOI (1935). The story, devised by Felix Adler, is a slapstick adaptation of "Pygmalion," with a couple of clever twists added. A wealthy professor bets a colleague that he can transform the Stooges into gentlemen within a matter of weeks. During this time, he gives the boys reading and dancing lessons, with hilarious results. The highlight of the film comes when the professor throws a huge society party in honor of his pupils. After behaving politely for a few minutes, the Stooges allow their instincts to overpower them and they turn the party into a melee of slapstick mayhem. Soon all of the party guests find themselves slapping, punching and poking each other in an orgy of comic violence. Repulsed by the behavior of the "hoi polloi," the Stooges leave the party in disgust.

This theme, pitting the Stooges against high society, turned out to be one of the most popular Three Stooges story formats. The script was rewritten more than a decade later as HALF-WITS HOLIDAY, with several new sequences added, including a massive pie fight. HALF-WITS HOLIDAY was itself remade, almost line-for-line, as PIES AND GUYS (1958), with Joe Besser in the Curly Howard role.

Columbia comedy writer Elwood Ullman says the Stooges developed quite a rapport with Lord, who was, at that time, their most frequent collaborator. Ullman recalls that story sessions between Lord and the Stooges were, to say the least, rather informal meetings.

"Del would be in his office, going over a script with the Stooges," says Ullman. "He'd describe the plot to them, saying ' . . . and then she makes the telephone call to the help wanted people, and you bastards come in,' meaning the Stooges. And they wouldn't bat an eye!"

In addition to their work with Lord, the Stooges turned out several shorts under Jack White's direction in the early 1930s. White's initial effort with the Stooges, ANTS IN THE PANTRY (1936), is one of his best. This one has the Stooges as exterminators who drum up business by bringing their own pests with them. The short was remade fifteen years later as PEST MAN WINS, with White's brother Jules directing and Shemp Howard playing Curly's role.

Jack White directed a number of Stooges films after ANTS IN THE PANTRY, several of which managed to capture the fast-paced lunacy of his first outing. His A PAIN IN THE PULLMAN (1936), which has the boys as pesty vaudevillians disturbing a trainful of their fellow performers, was a personal favorite of the Stooges themselves. Jack White received screen credit for writing as well as directing this short.

White's next short after the release of ANTS

A popular Stooges story premise has the boys as exterminators. ANTS IN THE PANTRY (1936) was the first of these "pest man" comedies.

IN THE PANTRY, HALF SHOT SHOOTERS (1936), has the boys accidentally enlisting in the Army. This short is significant primarily because it marks the initital screen confrontation between the Stooges and comedy veteran Vernon Dent. Dent had appeared in literally hundreds of silent comedies, working with such greats as Charlie Chaplin. He spent several years playing Harry Langdon's partner in silent comedies, and even appeared with Langdon when he was doing shorts at Columbia. In fact, Dent appeared with practically every comedian in Columbia's shorts department during the 1930s, '40s, and '50s.

Dent was an excellent foil for the Stooges, and his talent as a character actor enabled him to play everything from cranky landlords to mad scientists. Dent's stuffy characterizations often served as the foundation for a good deal of Stooges comedy.

"Vernon was like the mounting for the ten-carat diamond," says Jules White.

Emil Sitka, who worked quite frequently with Dent as a fellow supporting player, recalls that Dent was a very congenial man, very friendly and easy to talk to. Dent was indeed well-respected by his co-workers, and he remained among the Stooges' supporting players until the mid-1950s.

"Vernon was a great guy," says Ed Bernds. "And he was no youngster. He goes way, way back to the Mack Sennett days. Every once in a while I'll see a film clip from a silent comedy, and I'll see a young Vernon Dent! Vernon was a real trouper, a very hardworking guy."

Another character actor who worked quite frequently with the Stooges was Bud Jamison. Another veteran of silent comedy, Jamison enhanced many a Columbia short with his wide variety of character roles. Jamison had years of experience behind him, having worked with some of the biggest comics in screen history. Like Vernon Dent, he could play dozens of different characters, from tough street cops to prissy butlers. And, like Dent, he played each role with ability.

"Bud had died by the time I started directing," says Ed Bernds, "but he was the same as Vernon— very willing, and very hardworking."

Ironically, both Dent and Jamison were Christian Scientists. According to Jules White, Jamison died in the mid-1940s when he contracted gangrene and refused to have it treated. Dent, in turn, became a diabetic, but did not take insulin; he eventually went blind, and died in 1960.

Regardless of the characters they played, both Dent and Jamison always appeared as authority figures at odds with the Stooges. Both men continued working with the Stooges until the end of their acting careers; their combined contribution to the Stooges comedies cannot easily be ignored.

By the mid 1930s, the Three Stooges' supporting cast was pretty well established. A cast of regulars was formed, with Dent and Jamison the two mainstays. Other comedy veterans, like raspy-voiced James C. Morton and burly Stanley Blystone, appeared in the shorts as well. Character actors Cy Schindell and Eddie Laughton also appeared in dozens of Stooges comedies, usually in small roles. In the late 1930s, the Stooges even hired Laughton to serve as their straight man for vaudeville appearances, stepping into the old Healy role.

One of the finest performers in the Stooges' stock company was silent comedy veteran Symona Boniface. Miss Boniface was a truly versatile actress, and she often found herself cast in the Stooges comedies as a matronly society-type.

Described by Emil Sitka as "a wonderful person and a real pro," Symona was the ideal straight woman for the Three Stooges.

In addition to the newly-formed cast of identifiable "regulars," the Stooges themselves began to develop their screen characters into easily identifiable personalities. As the 1930s progressed, their characterizations became more and more consistent with each film appearance. Less emphasis was put on the individual antics of each Stooge, and more time was spent developing ideas and gags for the team as a whole.

Elwood Ullman describes how gags would be fashioned for the Stooges: "Moe was more or less the straight man to Curly, and between them they got most of the laughs. Sometimes we had Larry getting laughs on his own, too. Sometimes we had a melange of all three."

There was by now no disputing the fact that Moe was the definite "boss" of the Stooges. Moe had honed his grouchiness into a downright mean disposition, and his comic personality became that of a somewhat sadistic bully, almost a comic villain. He could fly into manic fits of anger at the slightest provocation from his partners. This, of course, made it all the funnier when his bullying backfired on him. And it usually did.

Larry, on the other hand, came closest to the actual vaudeville definition of stooge. He did little more than take orders and physical abuse from Moe, and react with either delight or disgust to verbal nonsense from Curly, depending on the situation. Occasionally Larry would make a smart crack, or would actually make an intelligent suggestion. But for the most part, Larry's contribution to the act was limited to getting pushed around by his partners and looking happy, unhappy, or confused about the situation at hand. Larry

The boys peddle "Brighto," a patent medicine, as car polish. Guess who owns the car? Vernon Dent and the Stooges in one of Curly's best shorts with team, DIZZY DOCTORS (1937).

played the bland sap of the Stooges, the necessary go-between for Moe and Curly.

Curly, however, had developed a character completely distinctive, one that would be imitated by dozens of other comedians. The most popular of all the different members of the trio, Curly's childlike character made the Three Stooges. While his partners were allowed their share of funny business, the best gags were written for Curly.

Another interesting aspect of the Stooges' gradual character development was the association between their personalities and their physical appearances. Moe's appearance, squat and stocky with the simple, sugarbowl haircut, reflected his character, that of the tough, stubborn simpleton. Larry's physical features, the slight build, frizzy hair and tube-shaped nose, complemented his diffident, cowering character. And Curly's shaven head, cheerful facial expressions and bulging belly were merely physical extensions of his innocent, cherubic character.

Their voices were equally suited to their personalities. Moe's gravely voice was perfect for barking orders and spewing forth various sarcastic remarks, usually directed at his partners. Larry's nasally, pessimistic mumble was well-suited to his dialogue, which usually consisted of, as Elwood Ullman put it, "incidental stuff." And Curly's high-pitched voice, embellished with occasional squeals and grunts, was the logical verbal representation of his comic personality.

As the Stooges developed their screen characterizations, the style of their comedies began to develop as well. Many of their early efforts suffer from a sluggish, ponderous pace. The Three Stooges based their comedy on fast-paced, cartoon-like action, and, basically, the faster it was, the funnier it was. Once the Stooges and their directors started snapping up the gags and speeding up the action, the Stooges shorts found their niche in film comedy history as some of the fastest, liveliest shorts ever made.

The Stooges quickly became known for their quick-paced, incongruous antics. "When I came upon the Stooges," said Emil Sitka, "they were unique, believe me. They were different. When they started acting, it was like electricity turned on all of a sudden. Fast tempo and farcical, the timing was split-second. With guys like Hugh Herbert it was what they said and how they said it, but with these guys it was what they *did*."

More than any of their other Columbia colleagues, it was Del Lord who helped nurture and develop the screen characters of the Stooges. Ed Bernds, who served as a sound man under Lord, has commented that the Stooges probably would never have survived if they had not had the benefit of Lord's comic know-how and experience. Ted Healy had given the Stooges little opportunity to develop characterizations for themselves, since he was practically the whole show. Now, of course, the Stooges were carrying the ball themselves.

By the late 1930s, Del Lord and the Stooges were turning out some excellent work; nearly every short they did together was a gem. Lord's DIZZY DOCTORS (1937), for example, is highlighted by a climactic chase scene in a hospital, which serves as an appropriately staid backdrop for the unbridled mayhem of the Stooges. The boys all but destroy the decorum of the hospital, manhandling patients, colliding with people in wheelchairs, and wreaking havoc with the hospital's elevators. Featured is some of the funniest chase footage the Stooges ever used. With the aid of some speeded-up photography, the short contains some wild sight gags as the boys ride up and down the hospital corridors and eventually out into street traffic on a runaway transporting cart.

CASH AND CARRY (1937), another Lord effort, is unusual Three Stooges comedy. The story has the boys digging for buried treasure in an effort to raise money for a crippled child's operation. Surprisingly enough, the scenes with the pathetic child are appealing; the Stooges appear to be almost human. The boys refrain from their usual quota of physical violence in their scenes with the child, and the result is, to say the least, interesting.

CASH AND CARRY has plenty of violent gags, but none of them involve anyone but the Stooges themselves. While violence was an integral part of the Three Stooges comedy, it was not a necessary element for them to be funny. The Stooges could get laughs from verbal humor alone, but, unfortunately, a violent slap or a poke in the eyes was often used as a convenient way of ending a particular bit of business. Close examination reveals that the best Three Stooges comedies are those that rely on farce, rather than sheer violence, to get laughs.

The pest exterminator premise first used in ANTS IN THE PANTRY was reworked for TERMITES OF 1938, also directed by Lord. In this one, the boys are exterminators mistaken for professional escorts. One of the writers of this short, Elwood Ullman, would later write some of the best comedies the Stooges ever made. During the 1930s, '40s and early '50s, Ullman turned out what are probably the best of the Three Stooges scripts, each brimming with hilarious sight gags and dialogue.

Like Felix Adler and Clyde Bruckman, Ullman was experienced and well-respected in his field. In addition to writing for the Stooges, Ullman's

Moe watches
Shemp's wife Babe
at a family get-together
during the Stooges'
heyday.

credits include work for Abbott and Costello, Martin and Lewis, and many others. He also had the opportunity of writing scripts for people like Buster Keaton and Harry Langdon when they were with Columbia. Later, in the 1950s, Ullman contributed screenplays for the popular Bowery Boys series. More than one critic has noticed the similarity between the antics of the Three Stooges and their younger counterparts.

Ullman points out that the secret of writing a Three Stooges comedy was devising one sight gag after another. "It was gags, gags, gags," he reflects. "If it didn't get the laugh, you cut it out."

Despite the fact that he contributed some of the funniest scripts the Stooges ever used, Ullman himself is not a particular fan of slapstick. Perhaps this is one reason why Ullman's screenplays usually included a good deal of clever dialogue, rather than simply one slap or poke after another.

While the Stooges did some of their best work

under the direction of Del Lord, another comedy veteran with whom the Stooges had considerable success was Charley Chase. In the 1930s, they began an excellent but short-lived series of comedies with Chase serving as writer, director, and associate producer. Although the Stooges made only five two-reelers with Chase, the quality of these films was significant.

Elwood Ullman says working with Chase was a happy experience, "He was a riot! A very funny man; bubbly and good-humored. He had Hugh McCollum on the floor all the time, roaring with laughter. We couldn't do any work!"

But it was in preparing a script for filming that Chase was absolutely top-notch. "I'd exhaust whatever I had to say about the script, and he'd say 'thank-you,'" recalls Ullman. "I'd leave, and he'd call his secretary in and dictate it himself—the whole script in one afternoon!"

TASSELS IN THE AIR (1938), a genuine classic of farce comedy, was directed by Chase from a script by himself and Elwood Ullman. The premise of the short concerns Curly's obsession with tassels—it seems his mother tickled him with one when he was a baby, so now he goes crazy whenever he sees one.

MUTTS TO YOU (1938) is another gem, with the boys as proprietors of a dog laundry complete with a conveyor belt full of screwball cleaning devices. The fun starts when the boys, on their way home from work, find what they think is an abandoned baby. They bring it home to fatten it up, and soon find themselves accused of kidnapping. A riotous chase scene between the Stooges and the police serves as the climax of the short.

One of the most memorable shorts the Stooges ever did was VIOLENT IS THE WORD FOR CURLY (1938), directed by Chase. The script was written by Chase and Elwood Ullman, and has the boys as service station attendants mistaken for three European professors. The highlight of the film is a clever word song, "Swingin' the Alphabet," which the boys and a classful of attractive young ladies perform at a private girls' college.

Charley Chase was a music lover, and he tried to work a song into his films whenever possible. His own shorts often showcased his singing voice, and a couple of his Stooges comedies feature music as well.

The Three Stooges developed a rapport with Chase that is evident in the quality of their films with him. Chase emphasized the farcical nature of their comedy, rather than violence and physical abuse; one can only surmise that Chase and the Stooges would have continued working together indefinitely had Chase not died in 1940. It is indeed unfortunate that the Stooges could not have worked longer with him; his vast knowledge and great comic talent were sorely missed in the two-reeler field after his death.

After Chase's death, his place as a director was more or less taken over by Jules White. In the late 1930s, White began directing as well as producing the Three Stooges shorts. Altogether, White would direct more than half of their Columbia comedies, with varying degrees of success.

Often considered a stern director, White maintained control over virtually every aspect of the shooting of a Columbia comedy. White offers his philosophy of making two-reel comedies:

"Economics entered into everything. The artistry of these things was one thing, but they were only as tall or as broad as their financial aspect. My artistic sense often said 'go for broke,' but my economic sense told me I couldn't afford to, actually. So, in other words, 'go as near as you can, but don't go for broke.'"

As a director, White often relied on mere violence to get laughs. In one White Stooges short, Larry tells Moe that he has had an operation and shows him the zipper in his stomach to prove it. The farcical gag is then ruined by having Moe sadistically, and without provocation, zip the cord up and down. The camera cuts to a close-up of Larry wincing in pain, making the gag all the more sadistic. The fine line between slapstick farce and outright sadism was often in question in many of the White Stooges comedies.

But White defends his use of violence for comic effect. "It wasn't so much violence as it was a *burlesque* of violence," says White. "The violence had a comedic undertone."

For the most part, White's early Stooges comedies were no more sadistic than any of the other two-reelers being produced at that time. Sadistic gags like the one previously mentioned were basically a departure from the norm in his early Stooges shorts. While violence was a mainstay of Stooges comedy, it was usually restricted to the Stooges themselves with the idea that the Stooges were not themselves *real* characters. Thus, any subsequent physical violence could not be considered real.

White's association with the Stooges would be a long one; today he has nothing but praise for them, personally and professionally.

"I liked all of the Stooges, and I had a lot of respect for their ability and cooperation," he says. "And they with me. If I said, 'Boys, this is how we're gonna do it. We don't have any more time to think about it, no more time to rehearse. Let's go out and shoot it,' there were never any arguments. They knew our problem. They also knew that if we spent too much money, we'd be out of business.''

White would contribute to the Stooges films as a director, as well as producer, from 1938 until their final year of production twenty years later. White's early Stooges shorts are all quality efforts, ranking alongside the work of Del Lord and Charley Chase.

As the 1930s drew to a close, the Stooges approached a new zenith of popularity. Their Columbia shorts had become increasingly popular with each passing year, and the Stooges found themselves in demand for live stage appearances throughout the country.

The popularity of the Stooges was such that numerous imitators and "other" Stooges groups began to surface. In addition to the Columbia trio, Healy's second Stooges ensemble had been appearing in shorts at Vitaphone, the forerunner of Warner Brothers, since the early 1930s. And there was yet another "Stooges" act, which actually called itself the "Three Stooges," also working in

Violence was inherent in every Three Stooges comedy, especially in those directed by Jules White.

movies. This ensemble had made some movie appearances at Universal Pictures. A couple of Universal comedies from the 1930s traditionally had been credited to the Columbia "Three Stooges"; recently, however, Leonard Maltin pointed out that the Universal trio was actually a different act.

The original Three Stooges' popularity was growing overseas as well as at home, so they embarked on a personal-appearance tour of Great Britain in the late 1930s. The Stooges claimed in a 1938 newspaper interview that they got the idea of "touring their constituencies" from President Roosevelt.

In 1939 the Stooges played the London Palladium, followed by appearances throughout Great Britain. Later that same year, the Stooges were contracted to star in a Broadway comedy revue, "Scandals of 1939," produced by George White. Many of the routines originated in that show, in addition to old material they had performed with Healy, and popped up in the Stooges' repertoire throughout the years.

The Three Stooges were so well-received on Broadway that George White reportedly contacted Harry Cohn at Columbia and asked permission to use the Stooges in his show for a few more months. Cohn refused, however, and demanded that the Stooges return to Hollywood to begin filming a new series of shorts. The new series included some of the best work the Stooges ever did, including adaptations of many of their vaudeville gags and routines.

For example, the Stooges had performed a sketch on stage in which they played famous dictators of the time. Moe's Hitler impersonation was put to good use in YOU NAZTY SPY, their first Columbia release of 1940. Even today the film stands out as a definite departure from the usual Three Stooges story pattern. And, oddly enough, it's one of the best comedies the Stooges ever made.

Director Jules White calls YOU NAZTY SPY his personal favorite of all his Stooges shorts. The film is full of outrageous puns and satirical verbal gags, but relatively little physical violence in comparison with most Stooges comedies. The emphasis is on verbal humor, rather than comic violence, resulting in what turned out to be one of the most different, and amusing, shorts the Stooges ever did.

White directed a number of Stooges shorts in which the boys are seen either as actual Nazi-types themselves, or simply as American servicemen at odds with the enemy.

When asked about these "Nazi" shorts, White says, "I think they were very clever and they were very timely. And extremely funny."

YOU NAZTY SPY was released more than a year before America's involvement in the war. Still, the short is full of biting sarcasm, aimed primarily at ridiculing Hitler's twisted logic and ever-increasing tyranny.

As the film opens, three ministers (played by Don Beddoe, Richard Fiske and Dick Curtis) of the mythical monarchy of Moronica are trying to find a solution to their country's economic depression. They decide that the only alternative is to create a wartime economy.

"But the Kingdom of Moronica is at peace," protests Beddoe. Fiske insists there's no money in peace and suggests starting a war. The ministers decide that they must oust the peaceful king and appoint a figurehead dictator.

"We must find someone who is stupid enough to do what we tell him," declares Curtis. Fiske nominates Moe, who is wallpapering Fiske's home with his two Stooge partners. Fiske introduces the Stooges to his two partners, and offers Moe the position of dictator.

"What does a dictator do?" asks Moe. Fiske explains that a dictator makes love to beautiful women, drinks champagne, and never works. Moe decides that he must think it over. As the camera cuts to a close-up of Moe, he brushes his bangs into a side part and accidentally rubs some dark paint under his nose, creating a Hitlerian moustache. Moe accepts the job, but only under the condition that his two partners are taken care of as well.

The three ministers decide to make Larry the Minister of Propaganda, and Curly the Field Marshall. "Can I have a uniform?" inquires Curly.

"You can have a *hundred* uniforms," replies Beddoe. "Just go out and shoot a hundred generals, and help yourself!"

Curly squeals with delight over the idea. "I'll shoot *two* hundred generals!" he shrieks.

Before long Moe is delivering a speech to a huge crowd of Moronicans. "We must throw off the yoke of monarchy and make our country safe for hypocrisy!" announces Moe. "Moronica must expand. We must extend our neighbors a helping hand; we will extend them two helping hands, and help ourselves to our neighbors!"

Moe quickly becomes obsessed with his newly-acquired power, and he turns into a ruthless tyrant. Disgusted with his tyranny, the Moronican peasants storm his palace. While trying to escape the angry mob, the Stooges make a run for it but wind up in a den of lions kept on hand to get rid of "undesirables." The closing shot of the film is a close-up of a lion licking his chops and belching contentedly.

The boys burlesque Hitler, Goebbels and Goering in one of their Nazi spoofs from the early '40s.

YOU NAZTY SPY was the first in a series of shorts in which the Stooges parodied the Third Reich. Moe performed his Hitleresque character several more times, while Larry, slight and scrawny, burlesqued Goebbels, and Curly, rotund and round-faced, represented the Goering figure.

YOU NAZTY SPY also initiated a series of Stooges comedies more consistent in quality than any of their previous efforts. The shorts the Stooges turned out in the early 1940s served as an excellent proving ground for Curly Howard's talents as well. With few exceptions, Curly is showcased in every short the Stooges turned out during the early part of the decade.

By the 1940s, Curly had developed into one of the finest broad comics in the business. His personality brought to the Stooges shorts a kind of comic "magic" that transformed many a mediocre film script into quality movie comedy.

Curly Howard has seldom received his due as a comedian, primarily because of the still-existing snobbery by many critics toward the Stooges' brand of humor. Lou Costello, for example, has been referred to as a "comic genius" by more than one writer. Jerry Lewis, in turn, has received similar accolades; many foreign critics have even compared him to Chaplin. But during his lifetime, Curly never received the credit he deserved. As the old adage goes, "Nobody liked him but the public."

Curly Howard never approached Charlie Chaplin in terms of artistry, perhaps, but he was nevertheless a highly original performer. As Moe put it, "He was truly a spontaneous comedian. In person, he was just as jolly and vivacious as he was in pictures—even more so. He was cute, lovable and kind."

Recently, however, several influential critics have pointed to Curly Howard as one of the most innovative and engaging comedians in movie history. Leonard Maltin has called Curly "a wonderful comic, deserving of far more praise than he ever received." Gary Deeb, in turn, believes Curly may have been "the greatest sight-and-sound comic performer of his day," calling attention to his ability to create "a genuine man-child character." Film criticism follows trends, and perhaps the breakthrough comments of writers like these will eventually launch a wave of acceptance toward the comic abilities of Curly Howard, and, subsequently, the Three Stooges.

It's safe to assume that the Three Stooges would never have become as popular as they did had it not been for Curly Howard's contribution to the act. He was a genuinely brilliant ad lib comedian, and his improvisation frequently greatly enhanced a trite movie script. Even in films that deliberately played up the talents of his partners, like YOU NAZTY SPY, Curly almost always managed to steal the show.

"One day Curly kept forgetting his lines while we were shooting a picture," said Moe Howard in an interview. "So he threw himself on the floor and kept spinning around like a top and making that 'woo-woo' sound of his. That became a regular part of the act."

In A PLUMBING WE WILL GO (1940), directed by Del Lord, Curly receives a good deal of screen attention. Many of the gags in this short were repeated in other two-reelers over the next ten years. As plumbers, the Stooges all but ruin an elaborate mansion with their working methods. Searching for a leak, Curly heads upstairs for the bathroom. He finds a leaky pipe and simply attaches another pipe to it, temporarily stopping the flow of water.

Then the water comes out of the newly-added pipe. Curly keeps attaching pipes, hoping the water will stop somewhere. Before long Curly has completely surrounded himself within an intricate maze of pipes! Curly finds an easy way of letting the accumulating water out; he drills holes in the floor, and soon the water comes pouring down into the basement. Eventually Curly drills so many holes the floor collapses, and he comes crashing down into the basement himself.

This short was remade by the Stooges in 1949, with some of the original supporting cast remaining as well as some original footage. Shemp Howard played Curly's role in the remake.

In FROM NURSE TO WORSE (1940), directed by Jules White, Moe and Larry persuade Curly to pretend he's insane by acting like a dog. The boys want to collect a fortune on Curly by swindling an insurance company. The premise is sure-fire, as Curly's character is pretty far from sane to begin with. Clyde Bruckman devised some excellent gags for Curly, such as the scene in the insurance doctor's office in which Curly chews the leg off of an examining table, and Curly's play for a pretty young woman in which he holds his "paws" limp, pants, and asks, "How about a date, toots?"

Lord's DUTIFUL BUT DUMB (1941) features a brilliant enactment by Curly of the classic "oyster" bit. The oyster bit is a wonderful piece of sight gag comedy, in which Curly attempts to eat a bowl of soup that contains a live oyster. The ornery oyster bites, spits water at, and generally abuses Curly for his trouble. This gag was originated in a silent comedy, and it was used by the Stooges several times in their Columbia shorts. Abbott and Costello even used this bit in one of their feature films. But Curly's rendition is the

Curly poses with his nephew (Shemp's son, Morty Howard) and his dog in these early '40s snapshots. Curly loved dogs, especially boxers.

funniest; the bit seems tailor-made for him. Curly's grunts and squeals hilariously complement the naturally funny sketch as he does battle with the oyster, eventually shooting it with a pistol in his frustration.

LOCO BOY MAKES GOOD (1942), directed by White, features a sequence in which the boys are seen repairing a dilapidated old room. In a hilarious bit of business, Moe pounds a nail into a wall with the back of Curly's head! Curly squeals in protest, but his anger turns to delight when he sees how well his head has served as a hammer. Like a small child, Curly changes moods at the slightest whim.

This short also features an excellent sequence in which Curly, wearing a magician's coat full of rabbits, pigeons, and so forth, creates a disturbance on a crowded dance floor. Jules White reports that Columbia actually suffered a lawsuit as a result of using the routine. Apparently Clyde Bruckman, who wrote the short, had a penchant for lifting old material, and he simply "borrowed" the sketch from another movie. Bruckman had originally written the sketch for a feature film starring Harold Lloyd. Lloyd took Columbia to court over the matter, and won the case.

This lawsuit more or less initiated Bruckman's downfall as a writer; he found it more and more difficult to find work as the years progressed. He eventually committed suicide in the 1950s, shooting himself to death inside of a phone booth in Hollywood.

Some of Curly Howard's best work can be seen in what is another reworking of an old comedy script, AN ACHE IN EVERY STAKE (1941). Written by Lloyd French and directed by Del Lord, the film is a reworking of a Laurel and Hardy short. French had directed the Laurel and Hardy version, and he simply rewrote much of the old material for the Stooges. In this one, the Stooges, as icemen, are faced with the ominous task of delivering a huge block of ice to a hilltop house before it melts.

First Moe orders Curly to deliver a chunk of ice to the house. After Curly runs the huge block up to the top of the hill, he realizes that it has melted into a tiny ice cube.

"We forgot to allow for shrinkage," explains Moe. This time he sends Curly up with two blocks, both of which melt into cubes. Then Moe has a brilliant idea: each Stooge will be stationed on the steps, and they'll relay the ice to the top of the hill! This works out fine, and Curly, proud of their accomplishment, holds the ice up to show his partners. The ice slips out of the tongs and breaks into tiny pieces.

Undaunted, Moe has yet another idea. They'll bring the icebox down to the street, load it up with ice, and carry it to the top of the stairs. As the boys lug the unwieldy crate up the steps, they rest on a landing for a moment. The icebox, equipped with wheels, rolls backward and goes crashing down the steep staircase.

Just then the owner of the house (Vernon Dent) comes walking up the stairs with a mammoth layer cake. Seeing the approaching icebox, Dent screams and heads back down the stairs. The icebox catches up with him, though, and after a loud offscreen crash the camera cuts to a shot of Dent, prostrate at the bottom of the hill, covered with cake.

The Three Stooges reached their performing zenith during the early 1940s. This period served as a time of unprecedented popularity for them, as well as a time of great Three Stooges movie comedy.

Elwood Ullman recalls that theater audiences would go wild with excitement when a Stooges short was flashed on the screen. Nearly every film the Stooges turned out during the early years of the decade was a gem; there were few exceptions.

Most film critics considered the Stooges comedies to be the very dregs of artistic achievement, but they were by now the hottest property Columbia's shorts department had. The Columbia Stooges comedies were often voted by theater owners as their most popular short subject attractions, in competition with cartoons and newsreels as well.

Although the short comedy provided the perfect medium for the exhausting speed of Stooges comedy, the Stooges themselves yearned to star in feature films.

Despite their desire to appear in the more expensive, more prestigious features, Columbia restricted the Stooges to work in two-reelers. Occasionally the Stooges made gag appearances in Columbia features, but for the most part, arch-rivals Abbott and Costello dominated the feature comedy scene in the 1940s.

Ed Bernds has said that Moe Howard was certain Abbott and Costello were actually stealing material from the Stooges. "I don't know how he knew," says Bernds, "but Moe told me that they regularly got prints of the two-reelers, looked at them, and in due course of time the routines, or the gestures, or the mannerisms showed up in the Abbott and Costello pictures."

As the 1940s progressed, the individual directing styles of White and Lord began to come into sharper focus. While silent comedy veteran Harry Edwards directed a couple of good Stooges shorts, the bulk of the directing work was split between White and Lord. During the mid-1940s, the two production units of White and Hugh McCollum

The boys as they appeared in CRASH GOES THE HASH (1944),
one of their most representative two-reelers.

also developed into significant rivalries. White continued producing and directing his own shorts, retaining Felix Adler and Clyde Bruckman as writers. Occasionally Jack White was brought in to collaborate on a script as well.

White's CRASH GOES THE HASH (1944) has the boys as newspaper reporters masquerading as servants at a society party. This film is significant in that practically every routine or bit of business the Stooges ever used is worked into the film's plotline. Surprisingly enough, most of the exclusively "Three Stooges" gags fit comfortably into the story. GENTS WITHOUT CENTS (1944) is worth watching if only for the Stooges' rendition of the burlesque classic "Niagara Falls." The bit, which derives its laughs from slapstick and a good share of violence, seems tailored for the Stooges. And NO DOUGH, BOYS (1944), a wartime spoof, features some hilarious acrobatics by the Stooges.

While White was now directing as often as he was producing, McCollum, on the other hand, worked solely as a producer. Del Lord served as McCollum's top director, with Elwood Ullman and Monty Collins, himself a comic performer, comprising the writing staff. And Harry Edwards wrote and directed exclusively for McCollum, although his work with the Stooges was limited.

Del Lord continued to turn out first-rate work with the Stooges. While most of the Lord shorts of the mid-1940s offer nothing particularly outstanding in the way of inventiveness, each is a clever entry in the series. PHONY EXPRESS (1943) is a fast-moving Western spoof with the boys mistaken for tough lawmen. BUSY BUDDIES (1944) features some good sight gags, with the Stooges operating a fast-food restaurant. And IDLE ROOMERS (1944) casts the boys as hapless bellhops who come to grips with an escaped monster. This short is especially noteworthy in that it is the first time the Stooges were seen with Christine McIntyre, a lovely blond who would appear in films with the Stooges for another ten years.

A protegee of producer Hugh McCollum, Miss McIntyre quickly became the first lady of the Three Stooges comedies. A talented actress, Christine was blessed with a marvelous soprano voice as well. Often her singing talents were showcased in the Stooges comedies. Christine's physical beauty and graceful manner served as an excellent contrast to the crude antics of the Stooges.

"Christine was great to work with," says Ed Bernds. "She was a real trouper, and very ladylike, but she learned to slug it out with the Stooges."

After the mid-1940s, Del Lord began working with the Stooges less and less. He was replaced, in effect, by Ed Bernds. Bernds remained at Columbia as a director for several years, maintaining Lord's tradition of churning out fast and funny Stooges comedies.

Bernds had wanted to direct films for quite some time before his opportunity came in 1945. He had served as a sound man for Columbia's top director, Frank Capra, and he soon became the studio's head sound technician. Working behind the scenes on the Columbia two-reelers gave Bernds a chance to study the directing techniques of men like Jules White, Del Lord and even Charley Chase. Bernds obviously absorbed quite a bit of knowledge from working with these men; the shorts he turned out with the Stooges were always of above-average quality.

Bernds recalls how he broke into directing the Columbia shorts. "Elwood Ullman was busy working at Universal, and Hugh McCollum was strapped for writers," he says. "He gave me writing assignments with the kind of assurance that when Harry Edwards quit, I would get to direct. In 1944, I quit as a sound man. I think it was when Roosevelt died in April of '45 that I directed my first picture with the Stooges. Boy, it was a great relief for me when Elwood came back from Universal and began to write scripts. He was very good at it and there was far more than I could handle."

Bernds enjoyed working with the Stooges, though. "When I came to direct them, they had already known me as a sound man," he says. "I had worked with them on their very first picture at Columbia. This might have worked against me, since they knew me up from the ranks. But they cooperated very fully, right from the start. It was a lot of fun working with them."

Emil Sitka, who appeared in a number of Bernds' Stooges comedies, says Bernds encouraged creativity and fostered a relaxed atmosphere on the set:

"He allowed me to create the character. And I could develop it to such an extent that it would be altogether my own."

Sitka adds that Bernds was a "very nice, genial" director. "Many directors are impatient, arrogant and stern. They won't repeat themselves," he says. "But with Ed Bernds you could work it out, reason it out. That's why I liked working with him the best."

This more or less easygoing directing style is reflected in the Bernds Stooges shorts. Good ad libs are plentiful, and the performances flow smoothly and naturally. Unfortunately, most of the shorts Bernds did with Curly as a member of the Stooges are marred by a lack of energy on

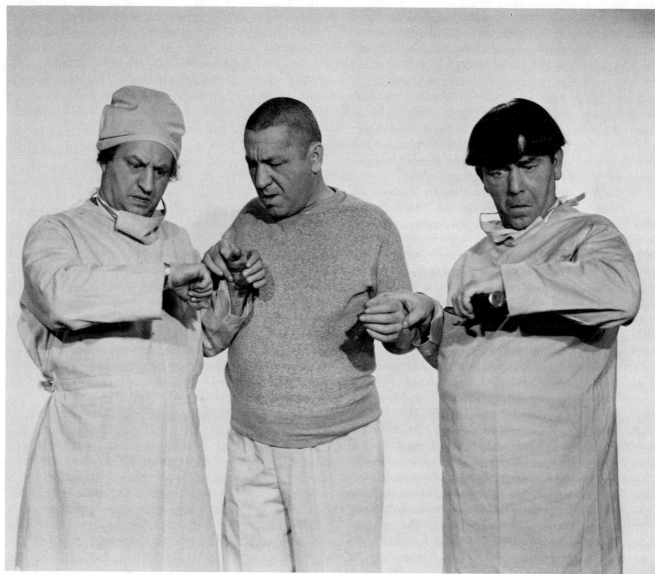

Curly, as he appeared after his stroke, in 1945. From MONKEY BUSINESSMEN (1946).

Curly's part. At about the time Bernds began work with the Stooges, Curly began losing much of his vitality and his timing seemed to grow slower with each performance. Although he was not well, Curly continued to make appearances with the Stooges, both on film and in public.

Curly's dedication, however, eventually caught up with him. In early 1945, on the same day President Roosevelt died, Curly Howard suffered a stroke. He was just 42.

Surprisingly enough, Curly resumed work with the Stooges shortly after his stroke. The Stooges continued filming their Columbia shorts, even though much of the comic load was now focused on Moe and Larry. Although he struggled to continue in the act, Curly simply couldn't recapture the vitality and elfish quality that had distinguished him as the star member of the Stooges.

Emil Sitka, who appeared in HALF-WITS HOLIDAY, Curly's last comedy as one of the Stooges, recalls that Curly was quite subdued after his stroke:

"Curly was really quiet, believe it or not. He surprised me, because he would hardly talk at all. He said, 'yes, sir' to everybody on the set and wouldn't discuss what he planned to do in the film."

Bernds says working with Curly after his stroke was a struggle. "By the time I started directing them in 1945," says Bernds, "Curly was a sick man. He was a very, very funny guy in his prime, but by 1945 he was not well. He couldn't remember his lines, and he was a little slower in his reactions."

The first short Bernds wrote and directed for the Stooges was A BIRD IN THE HEAD (1946), a pretty good offering considering Curly was very ill at the time of filming. This one has a mad scientist (Vernon Dent) after Curly's puny brain—he wants to transplant it into the skull of his pet gorilla. Because of his illness, Curly's actual screen time is limited. Bernds simply shifted much of the action to Moe and Larry, with better-than-expected results.

Bernds recalls that directing MONKEY BUSINESSMEN (1946), however, was a rather miserable experience. Bernds says Curly was so sick that he couldn't remember one line after another. Moe, however, helped out by coaching Curly on his material.

"Moe was great," says Bernds. "He worked with Curly like he would with a child, and somehow we got through it."

Bernds' best Stooges short was MICRO-PHONIES (1945). The film serves as a testimonial to the fact that, next to Del Lord, Ed Bernds more

fully understood the comic abilities and limitations of the Stooges than any of their other directors.

The script is a neat, flowing work loaded with memorable gags and routines from start to finish. The supporting cast is also top-drawer, with familiar faces like Christine McIntyre, Symona Boniface, and, in a hilarious character role, Gino Corrado. The short exploits Miss McIntyre's fine singing voice and features a number of musical sequences. But perhaps the film's most significant aspect, and another example that says a great deal of Bernds' directorial talent, is Curly's performance. Despite his illness and increasing lack of energy, he manages to turn in a funny, worthwhile performance, maintaining a good share of the comic burden.

Bernds began work on MICRO-PHONIES after A BIRD IN THE HEAD was completed, but MICRO-PHONIES was rushed into release first because producer Hugh McCollum wanted to impress Columbia executives with Bernds' talent as a writer and director.

The plot of MICRO-PHONIES has Curly masquerading as a female vocalist, "Senorita Cucaracha," in order to entertain at a society party. Moe and Larry appear as the Senorita's accompanists, dressed in tuxedoes and tails. All of this comes about because the Stooges, custodians at a radio station, "borrow" a record of Christine's aria, the "Voice of Spring," and mime the words themselves. A sequence in which the boys clumsily mouth the words to "Sextet from Lucia" is the hilarious highlight of the film.

MICRO-PHONIES was the short that won Ed Bernds his position as a full-time director. Bernds recalls that he wrote the script for MICRO-PHONIES at the request of Hugh McCollum. "I wasn't even aware that Christine McIntyre was a singer," says Bernds, "but after I'd done A BIRD IN THE HEAD, McCollum asked me to write something that would take advantage of her singing voice. She actually auditioned for me."

While the Stooges shorts were now blessed with an excellent new director, a talented leading lady and an abundance of good material, the films themselves were often severely marred by Curly's devastating lack of vitality. It was becoming obvious that Curly was a sick man; physically, he looked ten years older than his age. Curly no longer had the cherubic facial features and mannerisms that had made him so popular. Many of these Stooges comedies are almost painful to watch because of Curly's struggling, lifeless performances. In the hands of a sympathetic director, like Ed Bernds, Curly managed to turn in good work. Jules White continued to work with the

The boys in costume for their ''Maha'' routine, with Curly as the legendary ''Maharaja of Bulgaria.'' This routine was one of their most popular.

Stooges as well, although his work usually didn't match the quality of the Bernds comedies.

As Curly's energy sapped away, more and more of the comic burden was relieved from his shoulders. A good illustration of this is BEER BARREL POLECATS (1946), which has the Stooges as beer barons who wind up in prison. Curly is given relatively little to do, and a good deal of screen time consists of old footage of him from earlier Stooges comedies.

Occasionally, however, Curly was capable of carrying a good share of the comedy and was able to turn in first-rate work. In THREE LITTLE PIRATES (1946), for example, Curly is the focus of attention, and he turns in one of his best performances.

Curly performed his classic "Maha" routine for the first time on film in PIRATES, directed by Ed Bernds. Clyde Bruckman wrote the routine into the plot line, in which the Stooges disguise themselves as foreign merchants to escape the clutches of a sinister monarch (Vernon Dent). Curly's performance is top-notch, and, despite the fact that the film was made after his stroke, it's one of the best efforts in the entire series.

The highlight of the short, the "Maha" routine, is a clever melange of double-talk and nonsense patter. A running gag has Curly wearing a pair of bottle-bottomed spectacles that render him nearly blind, causing him to fall out of chairs and bump into walls. Curly's rendition of the myopic "nobleman" is flawlessly funny, and his timing and vocal inflections are letter-perfect.

This routine was adapted from a vaudeville sketch the Stooges had used since the late 1930s. The vaudeville version featured a knife-throwing sequence in which Moe assisted Curly in tossing rubber knives at human-target Larry at the opposite end of the stage.

Elwood Ullman remembers seeing the routine in vaudeville. He says Curly would throw the rubber knives out into the audience while Moe would attempt to straighten him out, much to the delight of the juvenile patrons.

Directing the Stooges comedies prior to THREE LITTLE PIRATES had been a struggle for Ed Bernds. "But by the time we did PIRATES," he says, "Curly was much better." There was hope that Curly would eventually recover much of his old comic prowess and return to the star position of the Stooges.

Little did the Stooges know, however, that their next short would be Curly's last as one of the trio.

Curly's final appearance as one of the Stooges was in HALF-WITS HOLIDAY (1947). The short, directed by Jules White, is a remake of their early comedy, HOI POLLOI, with much of the original script remaining intact.

This version, however, casts the Stooges as plumbers working in the home of a wealthy professor (Vernon Dent). Dent hires them for the "gentlemen" experiment, with the expected disastrous results. The only significant difference between the script of this short and that of the earlier version is that the climactic society party ends in a wild pie-throwing melee.

Throughout the pie fight, Curly is conspicuously absent; he had had a second stroke during the early stages of filming the party sequence.

Director White says the ending of the script had to be changed in order to accommodate Curly's absence. Moe recalled that Curly was relaxing near the set while he and Larry completed a scene by themselves. When the assistant director called for Curly, he didn't answer.

Moe went for him and found him with his head dropped to his chest. Curly was so stricken he was unable to speak. He had to be taken home, and Moe and Larry were forced to finish filming without him.

HALF-WITS HOLIDAY is a sad affair. Curly's performance is so sluggish one can sense he was a very sick man. Curly had tried desperately hard to continue working after his stroke, and this eventually ruined his health completely.

Although described by Moe as a man "carefree and humorous," Curly's life was marred by a series of unfortunate incidents. There was a hunting accident that occurred when he was a teenager, in which he shot himself in the foot. It left him with a slight limp and occasional intense pain. This becomes evident when watching his movie appearances; whenever Curly runs, his limp becomes quite noticeable. For this reason, among others, Curly drank a lot of liquor. And heavy drinking was a contributing factor to his initial stroke.

He also had three unsuccessful marriages. According to a report published by the *Los Angeles Times,* one of his former wives, Marion Howard, sued him for divorce in 1946. The *Times* report read as follows: "She said he had used filthy, vulgar and vile language; kept two vicious dogs which she was afraid would bite her; shouted at waiters in cafes; pushed, struck and pinched her; put cigars in the sink."

Curly had reportedly married Marion two weeks after meeting her. That marriage lasted less than a year.

Curly was a talented comedian and, as critic Gary Deeb has put it, "one of the most graceful comics of his day," as well as a man whose life was filled with tragic circumstances.

He was truly the star of the Three Stooges,

Character actor Emil Sitka, as he appeared in the 1940s. Sitka's first film with the Stooges, HALF-WITS HOLIDAY (1947), was Curly Howard's last as one of the trio.

and he has deservedly gone down in movie history as the most popular of the various members of the act.

After Curly's second stroke, his partners were faced with the ominous task of finding a replacement for the popular Stooge. Moe and Larry had considered breaking up the Three Stooges for good, but Columbia was insistent that they continue producing shorts under the "Three Stooges" banner. After all, the Stooges comedies were among the most consistently popular commodities Columbia had.

More than ten years later, a newspaper report stated that Curly's two daughters attempted to sue the Three Stooges for a share of the team's earnings. Their complaint was that Curly had "organized the group with his brother, Moe Howard and Larry Fine and that his heirs had the right to participate in the profits." The article pointed out that Moe Howard, Larry Fine and Joe DeRita, who played "Curly Joe" with the Stooges, were among the defendants. Eventually the suit was settled.

Moe recalled that after Curly's retirement, he and Larry were presented with many comedians as potential replacements, but none of them fit their requirements.

Eventually Shemp Howard was chosen to replace Curly. Shemp was already under contract to Columbia, and was starring in his own series of two-reelers at the time. Jules White, a close personal friend of Shemp's, had arranged for the series. Many of these shorts were remakes of early Three Stooges comedies from the 1930s and '40s.

Shemp, however, was less than eager to get back into the act. He didn't relish the idea of being looked upon as Curly's "replacement," and was well aware of the fact that Curly would be a tough act to follow. But Shemp had little choice in the matter; Columbia made the decision for him.

Press releases were issued stating how happy brother Moe and former partner Larry were about Shemp's return to the act. At the time of his reteaming, things were going very well for Shemp. He had dozens of feature films and two-reelers under his belt, working at several different studios simultaneously.

Shemp had even owned and operated his own night club, which provided an additional source of income. Upon arriving in Hollywood in the 1930s, he had borrowed money from brother Curly to open a club on Wilshire Boulevard.

"Shemp didn't want to be in the limelight," says Babe Howard. "So he named the club after Wally Vernon." But Shemp himself made occasional appearances at the club, often headlining the show with a comedy act of his own. By the time he rejoined the Stooges, however, Shemp had sold the club.

As one of the Stooges, Shemp fit in well, even though his comic style was remarkably different from Curly's. Unfortunately, Shemp could never quite overcome the public stigma of being his brother's replacement. Also, he did not fit in with his partners as well as Curly had. Physically, he appeared to be much older than them, and his voice was often indistinguishable from Moe's. Curly's natural vocal pattern was actually similar to Moe's and Shemp's, but he, of course, disguised it with his trademark falsetto.

On the other hand, Shemp had a few points in his favor. Even without a gag haircut, Shemp could get laughs through facial expressions alone.

"Shemp could be funny even offscreen," says Emil Sitka. "He was funny just to look at. He had a big nose like a potato, and slits for eyes. Anyplace he'd go, people would just stare at his face. They were fascinated by it."

Shemp could also act. He was able to carry his own weight as a solo performer, where neither of his partners could. Curly had made a few films of his own without the Stooges, but this work has generally been ignored. Most of Curly's appearances without the Stooges were with two other partners, basically substituting for Moe and Larry. Shemp, however, had little difficulty playing character roles, with or without support. Shemp was a bona fide comic *actor,* rather than simply a slapstick comic.

However, many people believed—and still believe—that the quality of the act slipped considerably after Curly left the team. Comic Benny Rubin, a veteran of vaudeville himself, appeared in a number of shorts with the Stooges. He is among those who believes Curly was vastly superior to Shemp, and he offers his opinion:

"Curly was the funniest, but Moe was a businessman. Larry was a musician. And Shemp wasn't a very good actor. None of them were very clever. They were journeyman comics, in the sense that they were told how to act something out, in much the same way that one teaches a little boy how to dance."

On the other hand, many of Shemp's colleagues believed him to be a very funny man. Bud Abbott, of Abbott and Costello, once called Shemp "the funniest guy in the business."

Often, however, Shemp's natural comic abilities worked against him. Babe Howard recalls that his talent actually hindered his career development.

"Lou Costello wanted to put Shemp under personal contract. Just to get him out of the studio!

Shemp was doing the Abbott and Costello features at Universal, and he got too many laughs. Costello told Shemp he'd make him a big star if he worked for him. So Shemp asked him for $3,500 a week, which was unheard of at that time. Costello didn't hire him, of course, but he still made sure that Shemp didn't get any more laughs. Practically every funny thing Shemp did in the Abbott and Costello pictures ended up on the cutting room floor. And that broke Shemp's heart, because he couldn't help being funny. He was a natural.''

Shemp appeared, although briefly, in several Abbott and Costello comedies, as well as some Olsen and Johnson features, at Universal. He also starred in some features at Columbia in the 1940s, teamed with character comic Billy Gilbert. Gilbert, a close personal friend of Shemp's, had established himself at the Roach Studios in the 1930s. Gilbert even turned up in some early Three Stooges comedies during their first year of production.

All in all, Shemp Howard has been a decidedly underrated comedian, perhaps even more so than his brother Curly. Even the staunchest of the Three Stooges fans often dismiss Shemp as a second-rate replacement. But the fact of the matter is that Shemp was not doing Curly's act, nor had he ever made an attempt to do so. He was simply adapting his already-established character to fit within the framework of an already-established act. To be sure, most of the shorts with Shemp lack that special magic of the shorts with Curly. However, replacing Curly Howard would have been a difficult task for any performer. Shemp Howard wisely chose to play the role in a manner that was comfortable to him, rather than try to be a "new" Curly.

Once Shemp was reinstated as a member of the trio, Larry Fine suggested that the Stooges give a percentage of their weekly paychecks to Curly. Moe and Shemp agreed, and all three contributed money to Curly during his illness.

Curly's retirement from the act was a turning point in the Stooges' career as a team. They would never again capture the lunatic quality of their films with Curly, but nevertheless would continue to produce quality, often hilariously funny, comedies for years to come.

Curly returned to work with his old partners only once, in a cameo appearance in HOLD THAT LION (1947), Shemp's third short as one of the Stooges. With a full head of hair and visibly thinner, Curly could easily have gone unnoticed as just another bit player if not for his trademark snoring routine, performed with a clothespin over his nose.

Curly's gag appearance was intended as a morale booster on behalf of his former partners. It was his final screen appearance, and the first and only time that Curly and Shemp Howard appeared together in the same movie.

Despite encouragement from his former partners, however, Curly was despondent over his condition. Larry Fine once said that after his second stroke Curly became very depressed over the fact that he would never again be able to perform and, as he put it, "hear the children laugh."

Moe and Larry did everything they could to cheer him up, without results. Curly became a resident at the Motion Picture Country Home, a hospital for former employees of the movie industry, and stayed there for six years.

After several more strokes, Curly Howard died in 1952 at the age of 49. He was survived by his widow, Valerie Howard, and their three-year-old daughter, Janie Howard, as well as another daughter from a previous marriage. Curly was also outlived by three former wives, as well as his brothers.

Although the Stooges would continue performing as a team for twenty more years, Curly's shadow would never quite be erased from the public image of the Three Stooges. He left behind a marvelous film record of some of the most unique comedy ever produced, and has gone down in movie history as one of Hollywood's genuine masters of the art of low comedy.

Changes in
Personnel and Style

Shemp Howard, in character. Shemp was generally acknowedged as the most "naturally funny" of the Stooges.

Chapter Four

Shemp Howard rejoined the Stooges in 1946, shortly after Curly Howard's second stroke. He remained with the team until his death less than ten years later.

Shemp's replacement of his brother resulted in some minor changes in the Stooges' performing style. Often routines and entire plots that would have worked well with Curly as the comic focus failed to come off with Shemp. But when in the hands of a talented director, like Ed Bernds, the new set of Stooges was allowed to develop a style that was in harmony with Shemp's Stooge characterization.

Jules White, however, persisted in employing the "living cartoon" style of comedy that was better suited to Curly Howard's talents. In the White Stooges shorts, Shemp is often forced to perform the same gags and gestures originated on film by Curly. This, of course, only resulted in the appearance of sloppy imitation.

Despite the fact that the Stooges lost much of their charm and inherent appeal to children when Curly left the trio, some of the best Stooges shorts are those that feature Shemp. A great improvisational comic, Shemp was often at his best when left alone to do his own thing. Emil Sitka recalls that Shemp's frequent ad libs would have Ed Bernds on the floor with laughter.

"Ed Bernds would fracture himself watching him. Shemp would go on forever until he heard the word 'cut.' And I mean he'd be funny every second of the time! Sometimes Ed Bernds would just let him go on, and he'd die laughing, even though he knew they couldn't use that much material in the film."

Jules White reflects upon his relationship with Shemp Howard: "A finer, more entertaining, more comedic man I never met. He'd keep you convulsed with laughter all the time with the stories he'd tell. And I don't mean jokes, but things that happened to him."

Ed Bernds considers Shemp to be his favorite of all the Stooges. "Shemp was a honey," says Bernds. "He was a very, very nice guy, a real trouper. He'd try anything; he'd work his head off. He liked working with me, and he really put out."

The difference between the individual directing styles of White and Bernds becomes apparent in viewing the Stooges shorts with Shemp. By the 1950s, the incongruous, noisy nonsense of the White comedies, contrasted against the structured plotlines and contextual gags of the Bernds efforts, serves as a significant evaluation of each director's style and ability.

Virtually all of the shorts the Stooges made during this phase of their career were directed by either White or Bernds. Del Lord made one short with Shemp as a member of the trio, and producer Hugh McCollum even tried his hand at directing, but White and Bernds shared the bulk of directorial duties.

There were a few minor changes in the Stooges' supporting cast during this period. Bud Jamison had died in the mid-1940s, but Vernon Dent remained with the Stooges until his retirement in the mid-1950s. Christine McIntyre and Symona Boniface continued to work with the Stooges as well. And tough guy Cy Schindell turned up in a few shorts, after an absence from filmmaking of

Moe Howard and Larry Fine, out of costume, welcome Shemp Howard back into the act.

several years, before his untimely death in the late 1940s.

Ed Bernds explains that Schindell left Columbia in the early 1940s to enlist in the Marines. Schindell told him that during the war he contracted terminal cancer. "A very pathetic thing about Cy," says Bernds, "was that he was doing films even though he was dying of cancer."

Schindell would appear in a number of Stooges comedies with Shemp, usually cast as a gangster or thug. Make-up was used to disguise the gaunt appearance that resulted from his illness.

Emil Sitka began working with the Stooges more and more as the years passed, usually in the role of an elderly scientist or crusty old codger. Sitka was quite adept at playing eightyish old men, even though he was only in his early thirties. A remarkably talented character actor, Sitka often added the finishing touch to a Stooges comedy with a clever characterization or bit of business.

"Emil was very good," says Jules White. "He could play anything. It's not easy to be able to play a gangster in one shot, and a governor in the next. But he could do it. And he did it very well."

Elwood Ullman points out that Sitka was one of the few supporting players for whom the writing staff would specifically devise character parts.

"I never saw him refuse to do a thing," adds Ullman.

Sitka remembers how he came to play the "old man" character in the Stooges shorts. "This is the story I got from Moe," says Sitka. "The Stooges were doing their vaudevillle act in a theater one night, and after they finished, a two-reel comedy was shown. I was playing an old man in that particular short. By the time the short came on, the Stooges had already taken off their makeup and costumes. They were headed out of the theater toward a coffee shop to grab a bite after the show. On their way out of the theater, they heard the audience howling with laughter. They had to go back and see what was so funny! So they went inside, and saw that it was my character that was getting all the laughs. They later decided they would like me to play that kind of character in one of their pictures, too."

Sitka worked marvelously with the Stooges, quickly becoming one of their favorite supporting players. Moe enjoyed his work so much he even asked him to become an actual member of the Stooges many years later. Sitka continued to appear in the Columbia Stooges shorts until their final year of production in 1958.

The first Three Stooges comedy featuring Shemp Howard as one of the trio, FRIGHT NIGHT (1947), was directed by Ed Bernds from a Clyde Bruckman screenplay. Bernds really got the series off to a good start; the film moves along briskly and is full of material well-suited to the "new" Stooges team.

The short is highlighted by a climactic chase sequence. In this one, the boys are fight managers who run afoul of a murderous gang. The gangsters take the Stooges "for a ride," kidnapping them to a deserted warehouse where they plan to rub them out. Tough guy Harold Brauer backs the Stooges up against a wall, and his men make ready to plug the boys. Shemp, however, pleads for his life.

"Please don't shoot me," he begs. "I'm too young and good-lookin' to die;" then, "Well, too *young*!" Shemp manages to drive most of the gang to tears with a sob story, as he names off all the members of his family: "I've got a father. I've got a mother. I've got a *grandmother*!" Then he starts in on his brothers and sisters, starting from the shortest brother and working his way up. By the time he gets to his "great, big brother," he slaps the gun out of Brauer's hand, and the Stooges make a run for it.

A wild slapstick chase follows, featuring a hilarious scene in which Cy Schindell, playing one of the gangsters, is knocked unconscious and propped up by Moe. Using Schindell as a puppet, Moe carries on a "conversation" with gangleader Harold Brauer.

In addition to Brauer and Schindell, the film features another "tough guy" who would appear with the Stooges throughout the late 1940s and early '50s. His name was Dick Wessel, making his first appearance with the team as "Chopper," the fighter the Stooges are training. Ed Bernds brought Wessel to Columbia for work in features and shorts; Wessel's huge size and tough personality made him a perfect foil for the Stooges.

FRIGHT NIGHT was remade several years later as FLING IN THE RING (1955), directed by Jules White. The "new" version was actually a patchwork of old footage from the original with a few new sequences added. The White version includes a subplot that has the Stooges working for a mob leader, who decides to bump them off when they doublecross him.

FRIGHT NIGHT is significant in that it shows how quickly and easily Shemp made himself at home as one of the Stooges. One of the reasons for this is, undoubtedly, the fact that Shemp had spent so much time in vaudeville as one of Healy's Stooges. In addition to this, Bernds allowed Shemp to play his Stooge character as he saw fit.

"He never used Curly's mannerisms," says Bernds. "He brought his own style to the act, but he did fit in well. Shemp had his own style of comedy. He was a very funny guy, if you let him

Emil Sitka, perhaps the most gifted of all the Columbia two-reel "players," was often featured in Stooges shorts with Shemp Howard.

alone. A lot of times I'd just let the camera run, just to see what he'd do. Sometimes we couldn't use it, but he'd never quit until I yelled 'cut.' It was a lot of fun just to let him go.''

Bernds and the Stooges worked in collaboration on all of their scripts, with Bernds suggesting the basic idea and the Stooges embellishing it with ideas and routines of their own.

After Bernds and the Stooges developed a story, it was then turned over to one of the Columbia writers, who wrote the screenplay. As a director, Bernds then completed the final draft, and made all necessary preparations for any gags that required special effects or stunt work.

"The hardest part," says Bernds, "was devising the original concept, the starting framework. The rest was hard work, digging for laughs, but getting started was the tough thing."

Ed Bernds credits Moe Howard as being "a reservoir of routines." Moe devised a good many of their story formats, recalling old sketches and routines the Stooges had used over the years. According to Bernds, however, Larry Fine's story suggestions were usually of little value. Although some of Larry's offbeat concepts were occasionally developed into workable ideas, Bernds says that Moe frequently and openly showed his disgust with Larry's lesser ideas. Moe would insult Larry, calling his suggestions "stupid."

Shemp, on the other hand, saved most of his ideas for the actual filming. These ideas emerged, basically, as improvisational routines.

Shemp was allowed a good deal of improvisation in BRIDELESS GROOM (1947), Bernds' third effort with the "Shemp" ensemble.

BRIDELESS GROOM is a tight, coherent comedy with good gags and dialogue. Supporting performances by character actress Dee Green, Christine McIntyre and Emil Sitka enhance the sparkling quality of the short, and Shemp turns in one of his funniest performances with the Stooges.

The premise of the film has Shemp as a bachelor music professor who has to get married within a matter of hours to inherit a huge sum of money. The plot consists of attempts by Moe and Larry to find him a prospective bride, and prepare him for the marriage proposal and eventual wedding ceremony.

As the film opens, Shemp is giving vocal lessons to Dee Green, whose horrible voice beautifully complements her homely features and obnoxious, but well-meaning, enthusiasm.

To make matters worse, Miss Green is infatuated with Shemp, and throughout the lesson she continually makes amorous advances toward him. Shemp still manages to conduct the raucous student, occasionally twitching and going into spasms of shock as she shrieks out an ear-splitting rendition of the "Voice of Spring."

The ridiculous elements of the situation—Shemp a professor, the horrible student singing classical music—make this sequence one of the Stooges' best.

But the funniest scene in the film comes when Shemp learns of his inheritance and prepares to propose to lovely bachelorette Christine McIntyre.

Christine welcomes Shemp the moment he knocks on her door, thinking he's her Cousin Basil. She hugs and kisses him, not allowing him to get a word in edgewise. Before he can explain he's not Christine's relative, the phone rings and the real Cousin Basil is on the other end. Christine reacts in horror and accuses Shemp of impersonating her cousin. She lets loose with a series of brutal slaps across Shemp's face, culminating with a stiff punch to Shemp's jaw that sends him crashing through the door.

Director Ed Bernds calls this sequence one of his personal favorites:

"Christine was quite a lady—she really was—and it was not in her nature to slap people around. We made several takes in which she just kind of held back, and they were no good. And finally Shemp said, 'Honey, do me a favor. Let's do it once, and do it right—go ahead and let me have it.' On the take that's in the picture, she really nerved herself up and she really belted him! I can look at old film a lot of times and see ways that it could have been done better. But that was one sequence that, in my mind, was perfect. The way we nerved her up to perform! The timing was utterly perfect. Damn! It was timed to perfection!''

BRIDELESS GROOM was a reworking of an old Buster Keaton feature, SEVEN CHANCES (1925). Clyde Bruckman, who scripted BRIDELESS GROOM, had been a gag writer on SEVEN CHANCES as well.

BRIDELESS GROOM was itself remade by Jules White as HUSBANDS BEWARE (1956), one of Shemp's last shorts with the team. The White reworking includes most of the old footage from BRIDELESS GROOM, with minor deletions, as well as some new footage with Moe and Larry as the henpecked husbands of Shemp's sisters.

Remakes became more and more frequent as the years progressed. Both the White and McCollum units began reworking old material, especially old scripts that had featured Curly Howard. Ed Bernds remade A PLUMBING WE WILL GO as VAGABOND LOAFERS (1949), with Shemp in the Curly role. It turned out to be one of the best in the series.

VAGABOND LOAFERS was written by El-

Emil Sitka seems less than pleased with the Stooges in this still from the late 1940s.

wood Ullman, who had scripted the original Curly Howard version. Some of the better gags were retained, such as the maze of pipes routine. In addition to this, a subplot involving art thieves was worked into the story. Kenneth MacDonald, a slippery villain type, and Christine McIntyre, also adept at playing villainous roles, were cast as the crooks. Emil Sitka and Symona Boniface turned up in this one as a wealthy couple who hire the Stooges to repair a simple leak. Before long, though, the boys have all but destroyed their elaborate mansion. By the time the Stooges have finished, water is spraying through nearly every orifice in the house, including the electric stove and the television set.

VAGABOND LOAFERS was itself remade several years later. SCHEMING SCHEMERS (1956), directed by Jules White, includes much film from the orignial, as well as some pie-throwing footage from HALF-WITS HOLIDAY. This stock footage proved to be quite useful, as most of the action takes place between the Stooges (minus Curly) and a few unidentified party guests. As a result, this film could be used again and again, with Shemp Howard, and eventually Joe Besser, stepping in as "Third Stooge."

Some of Ed Bernds' most frequent outings with the Stooges consisted of a series of "scare pictures" he did in collaboration with writer Elwood Ullman. One of the most familiar themes of the Stooges shorts with Shemp has the boys encountering murderous criminals or madmen in a spooky atmosphere. Often cast as detectives, these "tense situations" gave the Stooges the opportunity to spew forth an endless succession of lines concerning their courage, or lack of it. Sometimes the Stooges were not cast as detectives at all, but merely bystanders drawn into dangerous situations by the lure of easy money or a beautiful girl. Without fail, however, the Stooges found themselves in more trouble than they could handle, and spent the remainder of the film trying to devise a means of escape.

Both Bernds and Ullman consider the "scare routine" to be sure-fire for getting laughs. Bernds points out the appeal of scare comedies:

"We'd go to previews and we'd think, 'My God, we've done this before, there's nothing new in it! What can you do new with scare pictures? The audience must be getting tired of it.' But we'd put one of those scare pictures on and, Jesus, the whole theater would come to life! The audience would scream and holler; they never seemed to get tired of scares."

Bernds' first scare short with the Stooges, HOT SCOTS (1948), has the boys masquerading as Scotland Yard detectives. Passing themselves off as true Scotsmen, the boys are assigned to guard a cavernous Scottish castle. A hilarious chase scene highlights the film, as a trio of crooks chase the boys in and out of the castle corridors.

HOT SCOTS is especially memorable because of the beautiful castle set used throughout most of the film. Acquiring such a set for a two-reel comedy often depended upon the ingenuity of a particular producer or director. Ed Bernds was walking across Columbia's complex of sound stages one day when he discovered the massive castle interior, constructed for a feature film. Bernds simply thought it was too good to waste:

"I went in and got Hugh McCollum, brought him out and showed him the set. I said, 'Let's get a couple of scripts ready; when they're finished with 'em, we'll use 'em.' So we had the scripts ready. A lot of times you'd see a set and say, 'Let's do a story there.' But sometimes by the time you had the script written, the set might have been torn down. You had to be ready to move right in, because at Columbia sound stage space was generally at a premium."

To make good use of the set, scripts were prepared specifically to take advantage of the huge structure. In addition to Ullman's script for HOT SCOTS, Felix Adler wrote a script titled FIDDLERS THREE (1948). This one, directed by Jules White, has the Stooges as royal entertainers for Old King Cole (Vernon Dent). The script allows for some offbeat slapstick, with the Stooges acting out several nursey rhymes. One particularly funny routine, "Simple Simon Met a Pieman," features some friendly pie-tossing between Stooges.

Yet another Stooges comedy was filmed on the mammoth castle set. Ed Bernds wrote his own script for a short titled SQUAREHEADS OF THE ROUND TABLE (1948). This turned out to be one of the most charming of all the Stooges shorts with Shemp, as well as one of the funniest.

SQUAREHEADS is an excellent farce, superbly blending the antics of the Stooges with a coherent romantic subplot and elements of royal intrigue. This one even permits the Stooges, playing troubadors in medieval England, to play instruments and sing. The highlight of the film comes when the Stooges, serenading the royal princess on behalf of her commoner boyfriend, perform a comic reworking of "Sextet from Lucia." Christine McIntyre, as the princess, joins in the song herself. The sequence is clever and entertaining, and is even amusing to those who generally dislike the antics of the Stooges. After viewing this short, one wishes that the Stooges were given the opportunity to exploit their musical abilities more often.

Shemp rehearses a movie script with a little help from his dog, ''Wags.'' Shemp habitually memorized the lines of his co-actors as well as his own.

All three of the "castle" comedies were remade by Jules White in the 1950s. None of them, however, matched the originals in terms of timing, cleverness or overall quality.

In 1950, the production team of Hugh McCollum, Edward Bernds and Elwood Ullman began work on a series of Stooges comedies that, according to Ullman, constituted a banner year for Columbia's shorts department.

"We had a string there," says Bernds, "where we just kept topping ourselves."

Bernds directed several two-reelers for McCollum, all written by Ullman, that turned out to be the last really good shorts the Stooges ever did, even though the Stooges remained at Columbia for almost another decade.

Ullman recalls previewing these shorts in theaters surrounding the Hollywood area. "We'd preview at an outlying theater on a Friday night, and pack the place with kids. And it would be both pleasing and disappointing. Sometimes a routine would come on, and it would die. And you just couldn't understand why! But after having previewed it, you could do something about it. You could cut out the dead spots, speed the thing up, and improve it."

The first film in the series, DOPEY DICKS (1950), is a detective spoof, with plenty of verbal gags aimed at deflating the glamorous "private eye" mystique created by Hollywood. In addition to this, the film has some genuinely scary moments, much more so than in any of their other detective opuses.

STUDIO STOOPS (1950) is another good entry in the series, with the boys as pest exterminators at a movie studio mistaken for publicity experts. The boys go along with the ruse, and devise to have a lovely starlet (Christine McIntyre) disappear as part of a publicity stunt. Their plan backfires, however, when a pair of gangsters overhears their scheme. The gangsters actually kidnap the starlet, demanding ten thousand dollars in ransom. The Stooges attempt to rescue her, and before long Moe and Larry find themselves tied up while Shemp manages to escape by stepping out onto a hotel window ledge stories above the ground.

Bernds points out that this kind of comedy, known as "high and dizzy," was almost as certain to get laughs as the "scare routine." This particular situation, in which Shemp is seen wandering around a window ledge inside of a suitbag, was even reworked for a Bowery Boys feature Bernds and Ullman did several years later.

Bernds' personal favorite of all the shorts he did with the Stooges is PUNCHY COWPUNCHERS (1950), an excellent Western spoof complete with continuous melodramatic background music.

The boys play cavalrymen assigned to disguise themselves as desperadoes and sign up with a dreaded gang of cattle rustlers. Assisting the Stooges in their attempt to clean things up is helpless Elmer, played by former stuntman Jock Mahoney. The character is a hilarious satirical version of the Hollywood Western hero figure. Elmer is quick with his guns, but he always seems to miss out on the fight, either by forgetting to load his pistols or falling off his horse.

Mahoney performs a variety of breathtaking flips and falls, and steals every scene he's in. The short is full of physical mayhem, from the standard slapstick antics of the Stooges to the constant stumbling of "good guy" Elmer.

Christine McIntyre is featured as Nell, Elmer's girlfriend. One beautifully-timed running gag, in which Nell single-handedly punches out a number of lustful badmen, is the highlight of the short. As she wallops each desperado with her fist, she proves herself to be a true lady by finding a comfortable place to faint after each beating.

Throughout the late 1940s and early '50s, the Hugh McCollum two-reeler unit continued to turn out one good Stooges comedy after another. The White-produced Stooges shorts, however, began to slip noticeably in quality during this period.

A typical short is White's LOVE AT FIRST BITE (1950). The film suffers from too many protracted gags and not enough genuinely funny material. The plotline, such as it is, has the Stooges preparing to meet their wartime sweethearts, who are arriving from Europe via steamship. A series of flashbacks, in which each Stooge appears separately, takes up a good share of the footage.

An interesting White Stooges comedy from the early '50s is SELF MADE MAIDS (1950), with the Stooges playing all parts in the film. The boys play themselves, their girlfriends, and all other supporting parts as well. Through use of trick photography and doubles for the Stooges, the film even features a chase sequence, the highlight of the short. But for all the film's technical gimmickry and innovative ideas, the short simply isn't as funny as might be expected.

Another unusual, but successful, White effort is SCRAMBLED BRAINS (1951). This one, written by Felix Adler, has Shemp returning home from a private sanitarium. Shemp has been suffering from hallucinations, and he apparently hasn't been completely cured. He's fallen in love with his nurse, a homely, toothless wench much taller and wider than Shemp. Shemp, however, envisions her as a beautiful blonde. Plenty of good gags arising from Shemp's "seeing things" make this the best short White did with the Stooges in the 1950s.

By the early 1950s, however, Columbia was

By the 1950s, each of Healy's ''Super Stooges,'' or ''Gentlemaniacs,'' were still actively performing.

one of the few Hollywood studios that still maintained a shorts department. The two-reeler field had begun to wane in the 1940s and was well on its way out by the 1950s. With the future of their movie career relatively uncertain, the Stooges decided to take a stab at a television career with a weekly series. The Three Stooges program was to be similar in format to their Columbia comedies; regulars were to include Emil Sitka and Symona Boniface.

A pilot episode was filmed at ABC Studios in Hollywood before a live audience. Emil Sitka says the script for the initial show had himself and Symona Boniface as a wealthy couple who hire the Stooges to work in their home.

However, shortly after completion of the pilot, Shemp Howard decided he did not want to pursue a television career. At this point Mousie Garner was asked to replace him for television appearances with the Stooges.

"Moe and Larry were all for the series idea," says Garner, "but Shemp didn't want any part of it. So they were going to use me instead."

Garner had already been appearing on television's "Colgate Comedy Hour" as one of the "Gentlemaniacs." "Colgate" was a revue-style program that had featured people like Abbott and Costello and Martin and Lewis. The Gentlemaniacs had been seen on the show several times as well. Sammy Wolf was still with the act, while Bobby Pinkus, another former Healy comic, filled in for Dick Hakins, who had retired from comedy.

Despite the fact that arrangements were made to replace Shemp, the series idea was dropped by ABC. For one reason or another, the pilot episode never even made it to broadcast. However, the Stooges continued to make appearances on television throughout the 1950s. They reportedly appeared on Eddie Cantor's syndicated "Comedy Theater" in 1955, broadcast in color. Since prints of that episode are not available, the content of their appearance cannot be determined. A description of the show, however, indicates the format consisted basically of comedy and musical sketches.

For the most part, though, the Stooges continued to receive their greatest amount of exposure from their Columbia shorts.

Throughout the 1950s, remakes of earlier comedies became more and more frequent. ANTS IN THE PANTRY, for example, was remade as PEST MAN WINS (1951). The original plot is followed quite closely, but for the finale, director Jules White added the pie-throwing footage from HALF-WITS HOLIDAY.

Their next film after the release of PEST MAN WINS, A MISSED FORTUNE (1952), is a remake of another Curly short, HEALTHY, WEALTHY AND DUMB (1938). In this one, Shemp wins a television quiz contest, with disastrous results. The results are mediocre, despite the presence of such Stooges stalwarts as Vernon Dent and Stanley Blystone. Jules White, however, continued to remake and rework earlier comedies with the Stooges until their very last shorts in the late 1950s.

In addition to reworking earlier scripts that had featured Curly, White and the Stooges embarked on a strange series of experimental shorts in the early 1950s, most of which missed the mark in the laughs department.

Many of these experiments deviated considerably from the established "Three Stooges" brand of comedy. Apparently it was felt that audiences were tiring of the standard Stooges nonsense. While the attempt to freshen things up was certainly a noble effort, the films themselves were generally weak in terms of structure and comic quality.

The worst entry in this series is CUCKOO ON A CHOO CHOO (1952), a rather depressing effort. The boys work separately, which accounts for much of the problem. The short was intended as a spoof of A STREETCAR NAMED DESIRE, which explains some otherwise bizarre characterization. But as a whole, the film is a weak entry, with more unnecessary slapstick and general silliness than genuinely funny material.

It was becoming obvious by now that the Stooges were getting on in years, and were not as physically flexible as they had once been. By now all of them were in their fifties, and had begun dyeing their hair.

Until the end of their career, the Stooges maintained their gag haircuts. "They clung to the haircut idea," says Emil Sitka. "Moe had to have his hair down in the front, and Larry had to have his hair bushed. Of course, Shemp had to be different in his own way, with his 'split' hairdo."

Sitka points out that Shemp had a difficult time controlling his hair. "There was no way he could make his hair stay in place," says Sitka. "Before takes, he would comb it back behind his ears. He tried very hard to make his hair stay back."

Shemp, especially, looked older; he was well past middle age when he reteamed with the Stooges, and by the mid-1950s, he was almost sixty years old. In addition to this, Shemp's comic prowess had begun to slip. Like his brother Curly, Shemp suffered a minor stroke, and, although it didn't force him into retirement, it did hamper his performing style.

"Shemp had a stroke in 1952," says Babe

The boys as they appeared at Columbia shortly after Shemp's stroke.

Howard. "He was sitting at home playing cards with a friend, and all of a sudden, he just wasn't acting right. He was in a daze. We later found out he had had a cerebral hemorrhage. Afterward, Shemp never even remembered having the stroke."

Shemp and Babe Howard moved out of their North Hollywood home, and bought an apartment building nearby. "We filled it with show people," says Babe, "and we'd have parties until three, four o'clock in the morning. I was doing it to keep Shemp going, to keep him up. After a while, he was back working with the boys again, going on tour, doing the shorts, and everything. But he was never quite the same afterward. He was never a hundred percent perfect."

Not unlike Curly Howard, Shemp's lack of energy became obvious in some of the Stooges' later shorts with him. Fortunately, stock footage was used to take up a good deal of the Stooges' screen time, so it was not necessary to relieve much of the comic burden from Shemp's shoulders.

Around this time, there were some significant changes in Columbia's two-reeler department. Most of these resulted from the culmination of the White-McCollum rivalry, which had reached its peak in the mid-1950s.

Confidantes say White and McCollum had always shared a "mutual antipathy," and it eventually came to the point where one of the two had to go. Since McCollum had served as Harry Cohn's secretary, he had been rewarded the position of producer. White, however, had been the official head of the Columbia shorts unit since its inception in the early 1930s. When it came to a final showdown, White apparently had more power, and McCollum was fired. White regained complete control of the department in 1952, and from that point on, the production of the Stooges shorts became his sole responsibility.

As a result, McCollum's longtime collaborator, Edward Bernds, resigned from Columbia. Bernds continued his successful association with Elwood Ullman, and they were hired by Allied Artists for writing and directing work on the Bowery Boys feature comedies. All of these films included material similar to Stooges-style comedy. Some, in fact, had entire routines and sequences repeated almost verbatim, with Leo Gorcey filling in for Moe, and Huntz Hall playing the "Shemp" role.

"We even used some Stooges-like material in an Elvis Presley picture!" says Bernds. "Comedy is comedy; if it's funny in one situation, you can generally modify it so that it's funny for somebody else. Some of the sarcastic things that Presley said were roughly things that, say, Moe might have said."

But with Bernds and Ullman gone from Columbia, the quality of the Three Stooges shorts took a definite nose dive.

Remakes of earlier comedies became the dominant output, and there seemed to be less time for earnest experimentation with fresh ideas. In addition to this, the demand for shorts began to dwindle as double features grew in popularity. By the late 1950s, the Three Stooges had outlasted every other comedian in the Columbia shorts department.

The popularity of their films, however, remained relatively constant. Columbia and the Stooges were given numerous awards from movie distributors for the continued success of the Stooges comedies. For several years in the 1950s, the Columbia Stooges shorts were among the nation's most popular box office attractions. For short comedies, they were selected top moneymakers for five consecutive years, from 1950 through 1954.

Shortly after Jules White was put in charge of the shorts department, he made an attempt to capitalize on both the Stooges' continued popularity and the 3-D craze of the 1950s. White had planned to produce a series of Three Stooges shorts filmed in the 3-D process. He envisioned a whole new series of 3-D Stooges comedies, all of which would capitalize on the nonstop violence and visual action inherent in the Stooges shorts.

For example, conventional bits like the "poke in the eyes" were amplified by 3-D, with Moe aiming two fingers straight into the camera lens, representing, for example, Larry's eyes. What resulted, unfortunately, was weak, forced comedy that visually fell flat when not seen in the 3-D process. At first glimpse, the behavior of the Stooges appears to be exaggerated to the point of silliness. In one of these shorts, for example, Shemp stares straight into the camera and quivers his lips for no apparent reason, other than to exaggerate what audiences might identify with the Three Stooges.

By the time the Stooges began making 3-D shorts, however, the craze was already on its way out. Only a couple of Stooges comedies were filmed in that process. As a result of the experiment, however, the Three Stooges have the dubious distinction of being the only comedy team that made movies in 3-D.

Despite the lack of enthusiasm over 3-D comedies, a series of 3-D Three Stooges comic books emerged in the 1950s, featuring the "Shemp" character as "Third Stooge." The series started in 1953 and lasted five years, long after Shemp Howard's death. The comic books could be viewed by wearing a special pair of glasses enclosed with each book. Much of the artwork on the books was

College football antics from the 1950s. During personal appearance tours, the Stooges often took time out for publicity-photo clowning.

done by Norman Maurer, Moe Howard's son-in-law. Maurer would later become an important influence on the Stooges' career, writing, directing and producing their films in the 1960s.

Aside from the 3-D experiment, reworkings of earlier films utilizing much old footage became quite abundant as the '50s progressed. This may have been a blessing in disguise, considering Shemp's health and reduced level of stamina. The first of these shorts, BOOTY AND THE BEAST (1953), was a remake of HOLD THAT LION, with several of the original sequences deleted in favor of new footage. Curiously enough, Curly Howard's gag appearance was retained in this version, even though it was not integral to the plot and Curly himself had been dead a year before the film went into release.

Footage from HOLD THAT LION also popped up in two more Stooges shorts. LOOSE LOOT (1953), directed by Jules White, has the boys in search of a criminal who stole their inheritance. The remake version features almost half of the original footage from the initial comedy. TRICKY DICKS (1953), also directed by White, has the Stooges as police detectives looking for a mad murderer. Footage from the original turns up in this one, as the boys are seen having trouble closing some uncooperative file cabinet drawers.

Perhaps the most interesting aspect of the frequent use of old footage was that the Stooges were forced to wear the same costumes as they had in the original movie to "match" the old film. The Stooges wear practically the same costumes in all three '50s comedies, all of which were released to theaters consecutively!

By the 1950s, it had become practice for Columbia to take an old short, splice in a couple of new sequences, and release the film under an alternate title as a brand new two-reeler. Jules White explains that this practice was simply an economy measure resulting from Columbia's continuing budget cuts.

"They weren't entirely old film," contends White. "There was at least fifty percent new footage, if not more, with a different approach to it."

The most obvious reason for this rather confusing method of film production was to sell the old shorts as new ones. In that way, Columbia could charge theater owners its standard fee for new releases, rather than a lesser amount for reissued films. Such chicanery would never have been permitted in feature film production; however, few theater owners paid much attention to two-reel "throwaways." As a result, Columbia was able to continue this practice for several years, churning out "new" Three Stooges comedies that were actually little more than old shorts with a minimum of new footage.

Nearly every short the Stooges made with Shemp before 1950 turned up as a brand new short with a different title and some new sequences. Leonard Maltin reports that through the use of old films, Jules White was able to complete an entire Stooges comedy in one day by the late 1950s.

Elwood Ullman says producer White made an arrangement with him to obtain his writing credits for Columbia. Ullman had been asked to write a Martin and Lewis feature comedy at Paramount in the early '50s; this meant, of course, that he would require a temporary leave of absence from Columbia. White made a deal with him: he would receive the requested time off, under the condition that Columbia would receive rights to his screenplays for future use. Thus, Columbia was free to do whatever they pleased with Ullman's material, and he was free to go to work for Paramount. As a result, Ullman would receive no payment for any shorts that happened to use any of his old script material.

Ed Bernds was less than happy, though, when several of his original writing and directing efforts turned up as "new" films with directorial credit going to Jules White.

"Columbia used my old film, without my knowledge or consent, and I complained to the Directors' Guild," says Bernds. "Columbia was entitled to release them forever, with no residuals. But in using my film without giving me credit, they were violating the Directors' Guild contract."

Bernds eventually reached a settlement with Columbia for $2,500. In addition to this, Columbia was forced to give Bernds writing credit on films which were remakes of his original scripts. As a result, Bernds was credited with writing the "story," while the writer who concocted the remake version was credited with writing the "screenplay."

"I really didn't care about the credits," explains Bernds. "I just hated to see Columbia getting away with a bare-faced theft. It wasn't right for Columbia to get away with reusing the film the way they did. They butchered a lot of the stories."

But despite Bernds' complaints, Columbia continued to release the old shorts as new entries, later creating much confusion among viewers trying to discern one short from another.

Although most of the shorts the Stooges turned out in the mid-1950s were little more than new adaptations of old releases, occasionally a complete original was slipped into the output. GOOF ON THE ROOF (1953) was one of these. The script, concocted by Clyde Bruckman, consists of one slapstick mishap after another, as the boys at-

Shemp Howard died in 1955, bringing an end to the Stooges' best years of performing.

tempt to clean up their newlywed friend's house. The title is derived from Shemp's attempt to install a television antenna on the roof, which results in his falling through the ceiling and into the house.

GYPPED IN THE PENTHOUSE (1955) has each of the boys as woman haters, resulting from their individually disastrous encounters with the same golddigging girl. The boys work separately, with Moe as her insanely jealous husband, Larry her former boyfriend, and Shemp the hapless patsy who innocently becomes involved. All three Stooges meet at the end of the short, resulting in a slapstick melee.

One of Shemp's last shorts with the team turned out to be one of their more innovative entries. BLUNDER BOYS (1955) is structured around a "Dragnet" theme, complete with monotone voice-over narration. The idea is a novel one, and a welcome departure from the often-stale Stooges story format. It's also an indication of the influence television was beginning to have on the motion picture industry: here was a theatrical film that poked fun at a popular television series.

The basic plotline is pretty standard material, with the Stooges as police detectives assigned to catch a criminal (Benny Rubin) who disguises himself as a woman. The boys fail in their attempt, however, and are yanked from the force. The closing scene has the boys working as manual laborers, and Moe ends the short by imprinting the words "the end" on Larry's forehead with a mallet. The closing credits of "Dragnet" never looked so good.

In 1955, the career of the Stooges was running smoothly, if not hurriedly, and that same year each of the Stooges took some time off for personal pursuits. In November of that year, however, Shemp Howard suffered a heart attack. He died almost immediately, with friends.

"Shemp had gone out to the fights with some friends," says Babe Howard. "He was on his way home in the back of a cab, and was telling a joke. He was in the middle of lighting a cigar when he had a heart attack and died."

At age 60, the second "star" member of the Three Stooges was dead. As Curly Howard's retirement from the act had initiated a turning point in the Stooges' career, so did Shemp Howard's death. After Shemp's passing, the Three Stooges would never achieve the quality of comedy they had before. It was downhill from that point on, even though the Stooges were together as a team for more than another decade.

According to Babe Howard, she attempted to sue the Three Stooges for a percentage of their earnings several years after Shemp's death. She argued that during Curly's illness and forced

retirement all of the Stooges, including Shemp, had given a percentage of their weekly salaries to Curly for his contribution to the act. She claims that after Shemp's death, however, the Stooges did not pay a percentage to Shemp's family. Babe says that eventually the suit was settled.

Babe points out that Shemp traditionally received twice as much salary as his two partners. This was a precedent that had been set by Ted Healy, who considered Shemp the funniest member of the Stooges.

Shemp was a talented comedian who never really received the credit he deserved. His originality, cleverness and comic abilities have, unfortunately, been relatively ignored. He was a talented comic who helped establish the Stooges, but left the act shortly before they achieved worldwide fame. In addition, he had the misfortune of having to return to the act in place of an irreplaceable performer—even though it was actually Shemp who trained Curly in the role of "Third Stooge."

Shemp is, however, revered by those who worked with him. Babe Howard has fond memories of a recent Three Stooges "convention" held in Hollywood:

"They had a lot of people who had worked with the Stooges in movies up on a stage, answering questions from the audience. And they all talked about Shemp. They spoke of him with such love and affection, after all these years. I was very touched."

Shemp's death had a devastating effect on his brother Moe. Grieved by his passing, Moe wanted to retire the Stooges as an act. Encouragement from his wife and Larry, however, led him once again into conference with Columbia executives to find another replacement.

Moe and Larry first considered finding an actor who could effectively handle the role of "Curly." Curly Howard had been the most popular member of the Stooges, and it seemed a natural idea to cash in on this success. Their first choice was former Healy Stooge Mousie Garner.

"Jules White told me Moe and Larry wanted me to replace Shemp," says Garner. "They wanted me to come in and play 'Curly,' and they asked Columbia to put me under contract as one of the Stooges."

Garner was a top-notch physical comedian with extensive performing experience. He had appeared in every form of live entertainment, from vaudeville to night clubs, and had a number of movie and television credits as well. One of his most popular routines was his "professor" act. This routine had Garner, wearing tiny pince-nez glasses perched on the end of his nose, playing gag

Mousie Garner was considered as a replacement for Shemp Howard; he lost out to Joe Besser.

songs on the piano. "I will now play 'Tea for Two,'" Garner would say, "from the motion picture, 'Ben Hur.'" Garner would then proceed to pound the keys with everything from his fingers to his elbows, eventually throwing himself into convulsions of comic frenzy and falling off the piano bench in exhaustion.

Garner's versatile repertoire even included letter-perfect impersonations of all the various Healy Stooges, including Curly Howard. This was undoubtedly one of the reasons why Moe Howard and Larry Fine considered him for the "Curly" role.

But Columbia refused to hire Garner; they insisted on utilizing whatever talent they already had under contract. Columbia suggested that the Stooges use one of their own contractees for the role of "Third Stooge."

While Moe and Larry searched for a suitable replacement, preferably a "new" Curly, they continued to churn out "Three Stooges" shorts—with Shemp Howard as a member of the trio!

For several shorts a double was used for Shemp, seen briefly and only from behind. Although Shemp Howard was dead, Columbia continued to use the "Shemp" character as one of the Three Stooges through use of a double and a good deal of old footage. When it was necessary for the surrogate Shemp to contribute a line or two, the editing department simply referred to old film and dubbed in Shemp Howard's voice. Occasionally, the double was required to grunt a response in a deep, gravelly voice, apparently in an attempt to pass himself off as the real thing.

Fortunately, this demeaning practice was discontinued after only a few shorts.

Shortly after Shemp's death, Moe and Larry considered the possibility of continuing as a duo act, with no third member to round the action. In their last few shorts with the "Shemp" double, Moe and Larry had carried most of the comedy anyway, and they seriously considered doing a series of shorts as two, rather than three, Stooges.

Meanwhile, however, Columbia had found what it considered a suitable replacement for Shemp Howard. His name was Joe Besser, and he was already under contract at Columbia. Like Shemp, Besser had been starring in his own series of two-reelers when he was inducted as a member of the trio. Besser became a member of the Three Stooges in 1956, ten years after Shemp had stepped in for Curly.

Emil Sitka continued to appear in the Stooges shorts, usually in character roles. Sitka turned up in several of the "Besser" comedies.

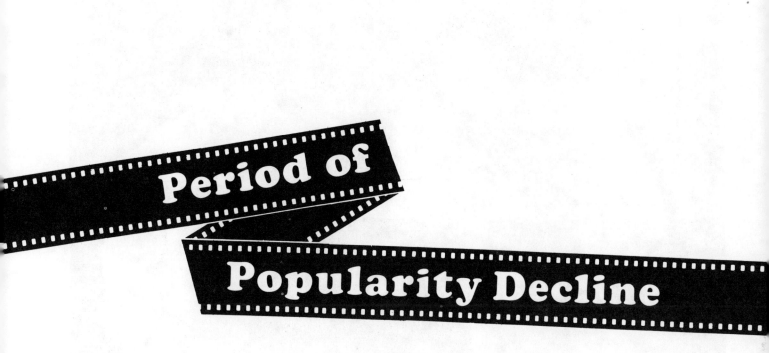

Period of Popularity Decline

Joe Besser (center) replaced Shemp Howard as "Third Stooge" in 1956,
ten years after Shemp had replaced Curly.

Chapter Five

Joe Besser was a talented comedian who, like the original Stooges, had received his training on the vaudeville stage. He had become famous appearing as a foil for Abbott and Costello, as well as Olsen and Johnson, and had a number of motion picture appearances under his belt. Besser was very close with Lou Costello; Costello managed to find movie and television work for Besser as a comic foil whenever possible. He may not have been Curly Howard, but Joe Besser came highly recommended.

Physically, though, Besser was similar to Curly Howard in many ways; he was short, fat and bald, with a cherubic expression and persnickety mannerisms. And like Curly, his comic character was childlike and patsyish.

"Joe Besser was a very cute man in his own way," says Jules White. "He had a lot of good gestures and expressions. And he was a cute little fat man to look at."

Besser says he was friendly with Moe Howard and Larry Fine, even though he was never close with them. He had, however, known them as acquaintances before becoming a member of their act.

"It was a lot of fun," says Besser, "because we were making people laugh." Besser was with the Stooges until 1958, when Columbia dropped them from their roster.

During this period there were some personnel changes in the Stooges' cast of supporting players. Vernon Dent had already retired from acting; shortly afterward, he began losing his eyesight due to diabetes. At Shemp Howard's funeral, says Emil Sitka, Dent had already lost so much vision that he had to be led to Shemp's casket by his wife. Dent's place was taken in a couple of Stooges shorts by character actor Milton Frome.

Symona Boniface had died in the early 1950s, and Christine McIntyre had left Columbia shortly before Besser's induction as a Stooge. Greta Thyssen, a pretty blonde, more or less took Miss McIntyre's place as the "first lady" of the Stooges shorts.

Emil Sitka continued to appear with the Stooges, however, usually in character roles. By now Sitka was the only performer who had played speaking parts with all three sets of Three Stooges. The size of his roles was beginning to increase in proportion with the frequency of his appearances.

Jules White continued as producer and director of the films. White's brother, Jack White, was still writing scripts for the shorts as well. Both men would continue to work on the Stooges comedies until their very last short in 1958.

Clyde Bruckman had died in the early 1950s, but Felix Adler was still employed as a gag writer. Adler scripted some of the better efforts in the "Besser" Stooges series.

But it was during this period, unfortunately, that the Stooges turned out what are generally regarded as their worst films.

Apparently a definite "style" for the new Stooges comedies could not be decided upon. In the sixteen shorts the Stooges did with Besser as "Third Stooge," the amount of experimentation with new ideas is mind-boggling. During this period, the Stooges ran the gamut from situation comedy to musical farce. None of these ideas ever

Mousie Garner was again considered for the ''Curly'' role,
in place of Joe Besser, in the late 1950s.

worked, although occasionally the results were interesting.

Probably the biggest problem with the new act was internal: Besser really didn't fit in as one of the Stooges. He wasn't Curly Howard, and he certainly wasn't Shemp Howard. He was Joe Besser, a highly individual and innovative comic. Unfortunately, Besser's character, that of a middle-aged sissy, simply didn't blend with the deliberately crude, brash behavior of his partners.

In addition to these difficulties, the Stooges were forced to experiment with different styles of comedy, ranging from comic fantasy to science fiction spoofery. Besser's first outing with the Stooges, HOOFS AND GOOFS (1957), is something less than top-notch. Oddly enough, character comic Benny Rubin is the funniest thing in the whole short. As the Stooges' pesty landlord, Rubin gets more laughs than the Stooges themselves— and that's something that never would have been permitted during their prime years of filmmaking.

The short is structured around a prolonged dream sequence in which Joe dreams his sister has died and is reincarnated as a horse. The gags are contrived and predictable, and the Stooges don't look too comfortable playing second fiddle to a horse. Despite the film's weak premise, a sequel of sorts, HORSING AROUND (1957), was released several months later.

SPACE SHIP SAPPY (1957) has the boys launched into outer space with scientist Benny Rubin and his daughter. There are a few moments of fun in this one, but, as a whole, the short fails to provide any real laughs. Strangely enough, two more science-fiction-themed comedies followed, neither of which show the Stooges to particular advantage.

One of the most interesting of the Besser Stooges shorts is SWEET AND HOT (1958). The script was written in part by Jerome Gottler, who wrote WOMAN HATERS, their original Columbia comedy.

Like WOMAN HATERS, SWEET AND HOT casts the boys as separate characters. Muriel Landers guest stars as an overweight vocalist who is afraid of singing in public. The short is not without fascination, but it's about as far off from "Three Stooges" comedy as one might expect. SWEET AND HOT is a situation comedy, with the Stooges simply splitting up and playing character roles. One might even suspect that the script was not written specifically for the Three Stooges.

Casting the Stooges as separate characters never worked, yet they continued to appear in films "split up" throughout their Columbia career. One would think that after nearly a quarter of a century it would have become obvious that the Stooges simply didn't make it as single performers.

In addition to these various experiments, several scripts from earlier shorts with Curly and Shemp Howard were reworked for Besser. Footage of Curly Howard proved to be quite useful, since Besser resembled him somewhat from a distance. Curly's last short as one of the Stooges, HALF-WITS HOLIDAY, for example, was remade as PIES AND GUYS (1958). This one turned out to be one of Besser's last Stooges shorts as well.

Since stock footage was being used so frequently at Columbia, producer Jules White could often turn out a "new" film in a matter of *hours*. Emil Sitka, who repeated his HALF-WITS HOLIDAY role in PIES AND GUYS, remembers how he was approached to do the part in the remake:

"I got a call from Jules White. He told me he was remaking HALF-WITS HOLIDAY with Joe Besser, and he wanted me to repeat my role. They even had my old costume ready. All they wanted me to do was take off some weight and read through the old script again."

Almost half of the Besser Stooges shorts utilized old footage to some extent. One of these shorts didn't even have a supporting cast; the Stooges carried the entire film alone. It was becoming painfully obvious that Columbia was no longer interested in what was once its top comedy attraction.

In 1958 Harry Cohn died, and, as a result, the Stooges were fired from Columbia. They had been the only remaining act in the shorts department, which was disbanded upon their departure. Jules White, their producer and frequent director for nearly a quarter of a century, retired shortly thereafter. The firing of the Stooges marked the virtual end of the two-reel comedy era, a sign that lengthier feature films and double features had firmly established themselves as part of the moviemaking industry.

Shortly after they left Columbia, the Stooges made plans for a "Three Stooges" personal appearance tour. Joe Besser, however, declined. He claims he was unable to tour with the Stooges because of a movie obligation in Hollywood. Besser says his appearance in the 20th Century-Fox musical SAY ONE FOR ME (1959) precluded him from continuing in the role of the "Third Stooge."

At this point, Moe and Larry began looking for another replacement. Once again, they considered Mousie Garner for the "Curly" role.

Garner was close with Larry Fine, who contacted him about teaming with the Stooges. "They knew they could use me," says Garner, "because I had worked with Ted Healy, and I knew the way they worked and the kind of material they did."

Garner was interested in joining the act, but at the time was under contract as a musical comedian to Spike Jones.

"I asked Spike Jones to give me a couple of weeks off to rehearse with the boys," says Garner. "He said that was okay so I started rehearsing the 'Curly' part with Moe and Larry.

"Moe had an office in Hollywood. We'd get together every day, the three of us, with me doing Curly's part. You know, with the squealing, and the barking, and everything. Moe loved it. He said I was a lot like Curly. So he told me to shave my head and start putting on weight."

But Garner was never to become an actual member of the trio. "I pleaded with Spike Jones to let me out of my contract, but he refused," says Garner. "Moe and Larry even went to his house, and asked for me. But he just wouldn't let me out."

In early 1958, the future of the Three Stooges looked bleak. Moe Howard was considering a career in the production end of moviemaking. One Columbia feature film from the late 1950s even credits Moe as an associate producer. Larry Fine, in turn, was considering moving from Hollywood, retiring from show business, and setting up his headquarters in his home town of Philadelphia. And Joe Besser, of course, had already begun accepting other movie and television offers. By the late 1950s, there was a definite discussion of officially disbanding the Three Stooges.

But while the Stooges themselves considered retiring their custard pie comedy for good, the "Three Stooges" was quietly on its way to becoming one of the hottest acts in show business.

Resurgence to Stardom

Joe DeRita (left) joins Moe Howard and Larry Fine as "Third Stooge" in the late 1950s.

Chapter Six

"Thanks to TV and thousands of young viewers, the Three Stooges are back on top."

That's how Robert Anderson, in his 1959 *Chicago Tribune* article on the Stooges, described the resurgence of popularity the Three Stooges experienced in the late 1950s. By 1959, the Stooges were suddenly back on top, and were well on their way to reaching unprecedented heights of popularity.

In a matter of months the Stooges were to become television stars and national celebrities. They would amass a huge audience of young children who had never before seen them in theaters but would soon be captivated by their slapstick antics. And, most important of all, the Stooges would form their own production company and finally get the opportunity to star in their own feature films.

All of this came about because Columbia's television subsidiary, Screen Gems, released a package of Stooges shorts to the television market in 1958. Columbia hadn't expected to profit very much from the old shorts, but within months, the Stooges comedies were among the most popular daytime syndicated television programs on the market.

While the Stooges themselves received no residuals from the showings of the Columbia shorts, the constant broadcast of the old films kept the Stooges in the public eye. Children across the nation became quite familiar with the antics of the threesome, and before long the Stooges were in terrific demand for personal and television appearances.

By this time Moe and Larry had found a replacement for Joe Besser. His name was Joe DeRita, a roughhouse comic who was also physically similar to Curly Howard.

Joe DeRita had been suggested to the Stooges by his friend Mousie Garner. "Joe was already fat," says Garner, "and he wore a crewcut. Moe met him and thought he looked a lot like Curly. So Joe wound up playing the 'Curly' part with them instead of me."

Although billed as "Curly Joe" for appearances with the Stooges, DeRita made no attempt to pattern himself after Curly Howard. This was a wise move, because DeRita had none of Curly's characteristic stamina or lunatic comic nature. The only major similarities between DeRita and his popular predecessor were that they were both fat and both had shaved heads.

Like Joe Besser, and Shemp Howard before him, Joe DeRita had worked extensively as a single. He even had his own series of two-reelers in the late 1940s at Columbia, the "Joe DeRita" series. During this time, DeRita was actually working in close quarters with his future teammates, turning out comedies which played up his cherubic qualities.

But DeRita had not known Moe Howard or Larry Fine prior to teaming with them as one of the Stooges. "I had met them years before," says DeRita, "but we were only acquaintances."

DeRita had started out in show business with a family dancing act in vaudeville, then moved on to comedy in burlesque when he went out on his own. DeRita was considerably younger than his partners, but physically, he fit in quite well as a

Even though he had been dead for years, Ted Healy's style of comedy still influenced the Stooges' act. They continued to use material from their Healy days until the end of their career.

Stooge. DeRita's character was basically gentle and relaxed, and, as Emil Sitka has described it, "cupid-like."

As a member of the Stooges, DeRita offered a pleasant complement, rather than contrast, to the characters of his partners. As the Stooges began to tone down their comic violence in the late 1950s and early '60s, DeRita's passive, less boisterous character blended in easily. Moe and Larry, both of whom were getting on in years, began to relax as well, both personally and professionally.

"Moe especially began to mellow out in his later years," points out Babe Howard.

This mellowing out was reflected in the Stooges' movie and television appearances. In the 1960s, the Stooges relied more on their established comic personalities than violence and roughhousing to get laughs. DeRita, in turn, played the "Curly" part in his own relaxed style. He simply adapted his own comic personality for appearances with the Stooges and often performed material originally written for Curly Howard in his own character.

"He never tried to be like the original Curly," says Emil Sitka. Sitka had appeared in some shorts with DeRita at Columbia, and recalls that his character was "somewhat like the one he did with the Stooges," but adds "he was thinner and he had his hair."

Sitka, who appeared quite frequently in films and on television with DeRita as one of the Stooges, remembers that DeRita had his notions as to how he wanted to perform. "If you were a director," says Sitka, "the best thing to do was to leave Joe alone. Because he wouldn't take suggestions. He ignored them."

Shortly after acquiring DeRita as a member, the Stooges began popping up on the entertainment scene more and more often. One newspaper columnist observed that there was seldom a moment when the Stooges *weren't* in the limelight, what with the constant showings of their old movies on television and their frequent live appearances in theaters and night clubs.

As the Columbia Stooges shorts grew in popularity on television, the Stooges themselves began making personal appearances throughout the country on local television stations that aired the comedies. The Columbia shorts were excellent publicity for them, and they capitalized on their renewed popularity to initiate a series of feature-length Three Stooges movies.

Moe Howard had wanted the Stooges to do feature films for years, but Columbia was reluctant to give them the opportunity. The fact that Abbott and Costello had starred in features no doubt had an influence on the Stooges' desire

The Three Stooges upstaged by a gorilla in a television performance.

to raise their status, both financially and "artistically."

For this reason the Stooges formed their own production outfit, Normandy Productions, in the early 1960s. The main thrust of Normandy was the production of feature comedies for theatrical release.

Norman Maurer, Moe's son-in-law, was chosen as producer for the company. Maurer would be the driving force of the Stooges films throughout the 1960s, producing, directing and even contributing to the writing of the features.

Normandy churned out several low-budget comedies in the 1960s, all of which are characterized by a low level of violence in comparison with their Columbia shorts. Even so, Normandy hired a number of the Stooges' former collaborators to work on the features. Elwood Ullman wrote the screenplays, and Ed Bernds even directed a couple of films. Several of the Stooges' former supporting players were even recruited for appearances in the films. Columbia distributed the new Stooges movies, all of which provided considerable profit for each of the Stooges. For the first time, the Stooges owned a percentage of their own movies, a full fifty percent to be split between them.

"Moe and Larry were very fair," says Joe DeRita. "Everything was a three-way split, as far as money was concerned."

But what is quite possible the best feature the Stooges did in the 1960s wasn't even produced by Normandy. SNOW WHITE AND THE THREE STOOGES (1961), directed by Walter Lang, was filmed at 20th Century-Fox on a budget of more than three million dollars. It stands as the most expensive Three Stooges movie ever made, filmed in Technicolor and released in Panavision.

Over the years the film has received a great deal of criticism from a number of standpoints. Many consider the Stooges' version to be an obnoxious bastardization of the classic fairy tale. On the other hand, many Three Stooges fans believe there's *too much* fairy tale and not enough Three Stooges in the picture. Most of the complaints, however, are unwarranted. SNOW WHITE AND THE THREE STOOGES is, in fact, a charming little movie. Critic Howard Thompson called the film "pictorially lavish, beautiful and tasteful from start to finish." He especially had kind words for "Ye Stooges Three," as they're called in the film, saying the Stooges, "never more subdued, are lively, to be sure. If their pleasant, friendly bumbling (the pies fly only once) doesn't exactly enhance Grimm, the boys do quite nicely as sideline sponsors of the hero and heroine."

SNOW WHITE AND THE THREE

STOOGES actually involves very little slapstick, but is an outstanding children's feature nevertheless. Elwood Ullman collaborated on the screenplay, which deftly utilizes the talents of the Stooges in an unusual manner. The film shows them to good advantage as sympathetic characters; the boys display an ability, however modest, for pathos that previously had been untapped. The scenes with Snow White, the Prince and the Stooges are tasteful and appealing. The film serves as a lasting testimony that the Stooges had the potential to develop into bona fide character actors in their later years.

For the first time in their movie career, the Three Stooges were beginning to receive critical acceptance for exactly what they were: low comics, but talented low comics nevertheless. Certainly nostalgia played a key role in the newly-found popularity of the Stooges, both with audiences and critics, and the Stooges capitalized on this phenomenon at every possible opportunity.

Ed Bernds recalls that when he began working with the Stooges again on their Normandy features, they had changed relatively little from when he had last worked with them in the 1950s.

"Moe and Larry were about the same," says Bernds. "Moe was a little touchier, and Larry was a little flightier. In their own ways, they were troupers. They wanted to do good. I guess Joe DeRita did, too."

Bernds notes that he was aware of the fact that the Stooges were no longer in prime physical condition. "Joe was very fat, and any fat person, if he runs or climbs upstairs too fast, could have a heart attack. And I was aware of that. I was also aware of the fact that Moe and Larry were a lot older than they had been before, so I tried not to strain them too much, either. For instance, if we had to shoot a scene of them running up a flight of stairs, I wouldn't ask them to actually run all the way up the stairs. We would do a shot of them running up a couple of stairs, and then cut to a shot of them reaching the top."

While age and size limited their physical flexibility, it brought the Stooges a kind of elfish charm. Seeing three aged men slapping each other and indulging in physical mayhem was grotesquely funny in itself. Even though the Stooges were well past middle age, this did not hamper their appearances. If anything, the ravages of age actually enhanced their physical features. Now Moe *really* looked like an old crab, and Larry's sagging facial features complemented his droopy personality. DeRita was much younger than his partners, but because of his girth, he still fit in well. As Moe put it in a magazine interview in the 1960s, "In color, we're just twice as ugly as in black and white."

A scene from one of the Stooges' television appearances.

Despite their comic stage appearances, Emil Sitka points out that the Stooges were very businesslike once out of costume, especially as they grew older. Sitka, who often accompanied them on personal appearance tours, says the Stooges more often than not resembled serious businessmen.

"After one of their features was shown in a theater," says Sitka, "the Stooges frequently would stand out in the lobby and sign autographs. But they usually weren't in costume. They had their hair all combed back, and they wore dark business suits. They looked very proper and dignified. Sometimes the kids were a little afraid to approach them. They looked really serious, even stern. The kids didn't recognize them without their makeup and haircuts."

In addition to feature film work, the Stooges embarked on a new and prolific career in television. The boys appeared quite frequently on the Ed Sullivan and Steven Allen shows, among others. They made a guest appearance with Frances Langford on NBC's "Sunday Showcase," and were featured in a number of sketches. On many of these variety-themed programs, the Stooges simply performed old vaudeville material from their Healy days, or routines from the Broadway show with Curly Howard.

They resurrected some old Healy material for an appearance on Milton Berle's show in the 1960s. Berle, a close friend and longtime admirer of Healy, stepped into the Healy role, with the Stooges reverting to their old "Healy's Stooges" status. Moe later pointed out that he really didn't like being on "the receiving end" of slapstick, particularly in this instance. While delivering a facial slap, Berle reportedly cracked Moe's tooth.

But the television success of the Stooges was tainted by one factor, still very much an issue in the television industry: violence. While the Stooges themselves had toned down the slapstick, the Stooges shorts nevertheless were loaded with graphic, visual violence, and parents across the country became outraged when their children began slapping each other and poking their playmates in the eyes. Many believed this was the result of daily exposure to the old Stooges comedies.

Responding to parental complaints, some television stations pulled the Stooges comedies from their program lineups. The general response to this, however, was negative, and station managers were sometimes forced to resume broadcast of the shorts. Many stations attempted to alleviate the parental panic by scissoring out the more violent gags, but the roughhouse slapstick remained intact.

On talk shows and in press interviews, Moe

Howard constantly defended the Stooges' style of comedy, explaining that it was all in fun.

"We're not as violent as we used to be," Moe pointed out. "Our comedy is based on upsetting dignity—something that's very easy for us to do."

But the Stooges did more than upset dignity. They became the scourge of parental groups across the nation, who persisted in their attempt to force the Three Stooges comedies off the television screen.

As a result of the outcry against violence in the early 1960s, the Stooges toned down their stock-in-trade slapstick considerably. They all but completely abandoned the "poke in the eyes," and at each personal appearance at theaters and in night clubs Moe would mention, for the benefit of the juvenile audience, that their mayhem was phony, that nobody really got hurt, and that it was all just for laughs. But he also warned children not to try the slapstick on each other, noting that the results could be disastrous.

Ed Bernds was well aware of the possibly harmful effects of the "poke in the eyes" while directing the Stooges as far back as the 1940s. Bernds was relatively tolerant of the often excessive violence inherent to the Stooges' routines, but he had his limits as to what he would allow to be filmed:

"Even as a fledgling director, I wouldn't let the boys do the 'poke in the eyes.' That was gratuitously cruel. I told Moe, 'If one kid, anywhere, pokes another kid's eye out, it's no good. It isn't that funny.' So in any picture I directed, there's never the 'poke in the eyes.' Jules White continued to use it, but I think eventually Moe himself decided they wouldn't do it. It's too real to be tolerated."

One of the Stooges' Normandy efforts from the 1960s features a clever self-spoof of their deletion of the eye-poking bit from their repertoire. When one character pokes another character in the eyes, Moe scolds him, explaining, "We don't do that one anymore."

Although violence became an important issue of concern for the Stooges in the 1960s, it was not a significant problem during the time in which they were actually making the shorts. Elwood Ullman describes the situation:

"We used our judgment and we had no particular trouble with censorship. As a matter of fact, when Moe punished Larry and Curly *too* bad, we'd get a general rebuke from somewhere. And we'd tone it down a little bit. Some of the methods Moe had were thrown out; they were too sadistic. We didn't want children going around practicing some of that mayhem on each other. And when Moe went around later on, making per-

The boys continued to make television appearances throughout the 1960s. This one featured them as Three Men in a Tub.

sonal appearances in theaters, sometimes in connection with the showing of feature pictures, he'd always caution the kids: 'Don't do any of these stunts, because you could hurt yourself. We did it for fun and we did it "cheating," really, but don't try it.' He always said that during the intermission with the announcements and speeches."

Ed Bernds explains, "Violence was our stock-in-trade, but we tried not to be senselessly violent."

Jules White believes the violent aspect of the Three Stooges shorts has been blown out of proportion in recent years. "My God," says White, "they've been doing violence in motion pictures since the inception of motion pictures. And it's been going on because it's a way of life. They want realism; they've got to take that with it. The trouble is that producers should tell these sob sisters to go to hell! Because they're the ones that create the trouble. Nobody was ever injured because the Stooges had broad-action comedy. Their form of violence was amongst themselves, and it wasn't so much violence as it was a *burlesque* of violence. If Moe slaps Curly and Curly says, "Listen, you, remember the good book says turn the other cheek," and he turns over and puts his fanny up in the air on a bench—that has a connotation of 'dirty.' But it's cleaned up because Moe kicks him in the pants, and he deserves it. There was always a provocation for the thing. Nobody ever just went into the scene and went "slap"; *never*. There was always a provocation for the slap or for the other things that they did."

In 1965, the Stooges completed a series of cartoon segments for television release, titled the "New Three Stooges." The violence was kept at a minimum, and the episodes featured live-action introductions by the Stooges themselves. In these segments, the emphasis was on dialogue rather than action; as a result, these sequences are rather weak. But while the live-action scenes are weak, the cartoons themselves, unfortunately, are even worse.

Released through Heritage Productions, the series was produced by Norman Maurer. Ed Bernds wrote most of the live-action episodes, and directed many of them as well.

Bernds explains that the cartoons were of low quality because qualified animators were difficult to obtain at that time. He adds that directing the episodes was rather nightmarish. Although he received reasonable cooperation from the Stooges, completing the live-action filming was a difficult task, even though the actual screen time of the flesh-and-blood Stooges was minimal.

Bernds personally disliked the series' format, that of the Stooges introducing the cartoons and

then concluding them with a quick bit of business at the end of each segment. He felt that switching from scene to scene without explanation was too unnerving for actors to comprehend. In addition to this, Bernds feels that the crew wasn't up to par, leaving him with more on-the-set worries than he really needed.

In 1969, Normandy began work on a series of color travelogs starring the Stooges. These were to be filmed in half-hour segments for television release. A pilot film was completed in late 1969, with the boys traveling across the country, pointing out the natural beauty of America's outdoors. The approach was decidedly relaxed, as the boys, supposedly retired from performing, tour the country and share its marvels with their viewers.

After the completion of the pilot film, however, Larry Fine was felled by a stroke in Hollywood. Since a series of episodes had now been ruled out because of Larry's illness, plans were made to release the film as a full-length theatrical feature. Nothing ever came of it, however. The pilot has been seen at various private showings, but even after ten years, the film has not yet gone into general release.

After Larry's stroke, Moe Howard decided to retire the act. Larry was taken to the Motion Picture Country Home, where Curly Howard had stayed after his stroke. Like Curly, Larry remained there for six years before succumbing to another stroke.

Larry's life had its share of personal tragedy (his son had died years earlier and Larry became a widower shortly before his stroke), but he often stressed that he was able to overcome his personal sadness by providing happiness to others through entertaining. Larry was also grateful to his daughter and family for their encouragement after he became ill, and he maintained a positive attitude about life even after his stroke left him partially paralyzed.

Although officially "retired" as well, Moe returned to occasional entertaining with appearances on local television programs in the Hollywood area, as well as several significant guest shots on Mike Douglas' syndicated series. One memorable segment of the Douglas program, and one of Moe's last television appearances, featured a demonstration by Moe on the art of pie-throwing. Douglas and several members of the audience, as a result, wound up covered with pastry.

Although confined to a wheelchair, Larry made appearances as well, mostly at local high schools and colleges. Ed Bernds, who attended one of Larry's personal appearances, says several Stooges films were shown, and Larry answered questions from the audience. "Larry spoke, but

By the 1970s, each of Healy's "Super Stooges" was still working,
although not together as "Gentlemaniacs."

his speech was slurred," says Bernds. "It was pretty grim. Having known Larry in his prime, it was a shock to me." Bernds adds, however, that the high school auditorium was packed to capacity with children and their parents who had come to see the popular Stooge. "I didn't realize there were so many Stooges fans," he says.

At the Motion Picture Country Home, Larry also helped organize stage shows and actually participated in the productions. Although his condition gradually improved, he made no attempt to return to professional performing. He simply didn't want to work himself into another stroke as Curly Howard had done years earlier.

During his illness Larry was persuaded to write a book about his experiences in show business. Titled *Stroke of Luck,* the book told of Larry's early days before becoming one of the Stooges, his experiences as a member of the trio, and his life as it was after his retirement. Larry even made television commercials promoting the book, which was published by a Hollywood company and sold on a mail-order basis.

Moe Howard, however, was less than pleased with the content of the book. "Moe had a very poor opinion of it," says Ed Bernds. Shortly afterward, Moe began work on his own autobiography.

Joe DeRita, meanwhile, continued making appearances, even though his eyesight was failing and his physical size had increased to the point where he was often uncomfortable performing. He made appearances at some local Three Stooges film festivals, where he was invited as guest of honor. DeRita even formed a comedy act of his own several years after Moe Howard retired the Three Stooges.

Strange as it may seem, the Three Stooges may have reached their peak of popularity years after the act had disbanded. A whole generation of fans who had more or less grown up with the Stooges through daily television viewing came to feel as if the Stooges were old friends. The demand for Three Stooges comedies never diminished, for theater showings as well as television broadcast. To this day, in fact, the Columbia shorts are still matinee staples at many theaters across the country.

While the "Three Stooges" had retired as an act, each of Healy's "Super Stooges" from the 1930s was still actively performing, although not together as a team. They had lost interest in working as a trio shortly after Healy's death, and had gone their separate ways. Occasionally they got together for local appearances in the Hollywood area, but they appeared primarily as solo performers.

Jack Wolf had retired from show business shortly before Healy's death. Wolf married and had decided to start a family, and felt that the hectic atmosphere of vaudeville would be unfit for raising children. Wolf's son, Warner Wolf, eventually went into a branch of the entertainment business himself; Warner Wolf is currently a television sportscaster. Jack Wolf died of cancer in 1964, but his replacement, Sammy Wolf, was still performing his comedy act in night clubs and revival shows throughout the 1970s.

Dick Hakins had also lost interest in appearing as a Stooge shortly after Healy died, but continued writing and performing as a musician. Hakins eventually set up his own recording company, and turned out a number of hit singles. By the 1970s Hakins was still active, composing music and working quite frequently as a performer in the Hollywood area.

Mousie Garner had also been working steadily as both a comic and musician since Healy's death. By the 1970s, he had dozens of movie and television appearances under his belt, as well as innumerable stage credits. Like his former partners, Garner was still performing at various clubs and theaters in Hollywood and the surrounding area.

All three of these former Healy Stooges are still alive and well and living in the Hollywood area, as of the writing of this book. Of all the various Stooges acts, these three men have the distinction of being the only surviving members of the original Healy Stooges.

Healy's "Super Stooges" continued performing throughout the 1970s. Meanwhile, public interest in the "Three Stooges" continued as strongly as ever. Moe Howard eventually became a lecturer on the college circuit, showing old Columbia Stooges shorts and answering questions from the student audiences about the team. Often he performed old vaudeville material, reciting the parts of all Three Stooges himself. Moe was still in demand for television talk shows, and he continued to appear on local programs. He even signed with an agent in hopes of obtaining movie roles as a solo character performer.

Moe continued to answer fan mail by hand, as did both Larry Fine and Joe DeRita. Mail for the Stooges never stopped pouring in, even after they had been retired from performing for years.

By the mid-1970s, the popularity of the Stooges was such that plans were made to bring back the team for a special appearance.

Problems arose immediately. Moe Howard had been retired for several years, and his wife did not want him actively performing again. Larry Fine, in turn, was physically unable to perform because of his stroke. And Joe DeRita's failing eyesight hindered him as well. However, after

Emil Sitka was brought into the act as a replacement for Larry Fine. He was contracted with Moe Howard and Joe DeRita to appear in a feature film in the 1970s.

lengthy consideration, Moe decided to resurrect the act—even if it meant bringing in a new partner to replace Larry Fine.

The "Third Stooge" had been replaced three times, so why not replace the "Middle Stooge" as well? Moe was confident audiences would accept a "Three Stooges" with only one of the original members remaining, and began making plans for the new act.

Obviously, the new member of the act would have to be someone familiar with the Three Stooges' style of comedy. Moe did not wish to rehearse a new performer for the role, and was looking for someone who already knew their act. In addition, the new member would have to be someone familiar to Three Stooges fans. There was little time for breaking in a new member of the Stooges.

Emil Sitka was eventually chosen to replace Larry Fine, primarily because of his comic acting ability and his lengthy association with the Stooges comedies.

"I was kind of taken aback, being asked to be a Stooge," says Sitka, "because then I'd have to forget everything else; I'd be typed as a Stooge."

But Sitka agreed to become an actual member of the team, and he quickly began developing his Stooge character. He was determined to play the role his own way, rather than attempt to imitate Larry Fine. His character was to be, as Sitka himself describes it, "conscientious to the point of being ridiculous."

Press releases were issued and publicity photos were taken in Hollywood of the new trio, as the "Three Stooges" were again signed to star in a feature comedy. The movie, to be produced by an independent producer, was to be dubbed in several languages and released throughout the world. There was also talk of an entire new series of Three Stooges comedies. But more problems arose, this time legal, and the initial film was never made.

However, the formation of the "new" Three Stooges had aroused public interest in the act. The group planned to make other appearances, and was soon contracted for a guest shot in a feature comedy, BLAZING STEWARDESSES, also an independent production.

Emil Sitka recalls that trying to get Moe Howard to rehearse the new act was no easy task. "If Moe was here right now," says Sitka, "he'd say we could wing it without rehearsal. Moe felt that we could make a scene right on the spot, that we didn't need to rehearse. And I wondered if we shouldn't have, because we were only appearing in a few scenes. It wasn't a Stooges comedy. But Moe, of course, assured me that we could do without it."

Then Larry Fine suffered a second stroke and fell into a coma in early 1975. A week later, he was dead. This devastated Moe, who was now the only living member of the original threesome. Moe nevertheless planned to go through with the new movie deal, but was forced to pull out when he fell ill himself.

"I had my bags all packed and was set to go film on location," says Emil Sitka, "and then I received a call that Moe was too sick to do the picture." It was later learned that Moe was suffering from stomach cancer, and he was hospitalized immediately.

Moe's illness precluded any further plans for the "new" Three Stooges. The team disbanded almost as quickly as it was formed. After a good deal of media fanfare and publicity, the return of the Three Stooges to the big screen faded into the realm of "things that might have been."

Perhaps the most interesting "Three Stooges" capitalization was a brand new "Three Stooges" act, which surfaced several years ago. Joe DeRita formed the team, called the "New Three Stooges." Another member of the act was Mousie Garner, who simply adapted his own night club act for appearances with the new ensemble. Moe Howard was still alive when the act was formed, and he was asked to tour with the new group.

"But Moe wouldn't," says Garner, "because his wife didn't want him to. She thought he was too old."

DeRita received permission from Moe Howard to use the "Three Stooges" name. "When we were putting the act together," says Garner, "we went over to Moe's house and asked his permission to use the title. He said it was okay, and then we asked him what percentage of the profits he wanted for letting us use it. He said, 'I don't want anything. I don't need the money.' I looked around at the beautiful house he had, and I said, 'With this house, you're damn right you don't need the money!'"

Since Moe refused to tour with the act, DeRita hired another performer to stand in as the team's traditional antagonist figure. Frank Mitchell, who had been part of a roughhouse vaudeville act similar in content to the Three Stooges, was hired as Moe's replacement.

The new trio opened in Boston in 1975. "The place we were playing was packed," says Garner. "We were pretty nervous, because we didn't know how we would go over, not being the real Three Stooges. But it went over great. I'd even say we were a smash. The audience was happy to see anything that resembled the Stooges."

The "New Three Stooges" featured a good deal of musical comedy, with Garner doing a variation of his "professor" piano routine. "Every time I hit a wrong note, Mitchell would give me a slap," says Garner. "Mitchell knew how to slap because his old vaudeville act was all physical comedy, like the Stooges."

The act played several engagements, but was forced to disband because of Joe DeRita's failing eyesight. This, combined with his large size, made it difficult for him to continue performing. "Joe couldn't get around very well," says Mousie Garner, "so we had to break up the act."

Shortly after the "New Three Stooges" disbanded, Moe Howard died. At the time of his death, he was transcribing his memoirs. These were later released as his autobiography.

At the time of Moe's death, television stations throughout the country announced the news, accompanied by film clips of the Stooges with Curly Howard. The last of the original "Three Stooges" was dead, and with him died one of the most memorable acts in the history of screen comedy.

Emil Sitka even gets into the nostalgia act. Sitka, himself a Stooges fan, still receives great quantities of fan mail from all over the country.

A Growing Constituency

Chapter Seven

Although most of the various "Stooges" are now gone, the "Three Stooges" comedy team, as perpetuated by the various media, is riding high on a crest of unprecedented popularity. As a result of the nostalgia craze, the Three Stooges have entered the 1980s more popular than ever.

The Three Stooges have never received more recognition than they are getting right now, the year of their Golden Anniversary. Film rental services report that the Columbia Stooges shorts are still constantly in demand. This is in spite of the fact, of course, that these very same films are being shown on television in dozens of markets, including the three biggest in the nation. These old movies are now approaching a quarter of a century of release time to television alone.

It seems ironic that years after the team has disbanded, and all of its original members are dead, the Three Stooges are quite possibly the most popular comedy team in America today. Laurel and Hardy and Abbott and Costello are still popular, to be sure, but their popularity has seemed to diminish in the last few years. It now appears that the Three Stooges, for years considered to be bottom of the barrel, are finally seeing their place in the sun.

And the Stooges are beginning to receive critical acknowledgement as well. Critic Leonard Maltin has written numerous books and articles in which he recognizes the Stooges, as he put it in one piece, as "truly fine clowns." Maltin has led the crusade in the last decade to abandon artistic pretensions and evaluate the Three Stooges on their own terms. Many discriminating viewers are beginning to judge the Stooges simply on the basis of their ability to provide laughs, without regard to "artistic contribution."

The Three Stooges have long been lambasted as being too "crude" to warrant critical recognition in movie history. However, many critics are coming to realize, finally, that that is precisely what the Stooges were *trying* to do. The essence of their comedy is outrageous crudity, and this concept was exemplified both verbally and visually. As Leonard Maltin has put it, "Their 'artlessness' is their particular 'art.'"

In a recent newspaper article on the Stooges, Greg Daugherty noted that "foes and fans alike are impressed by the trio's staying power," adding that "though they sent their first pies aloft nearly half a century ago, they still remain popular."

Gary Deeb recently confessed his love for the trio. "I'm not ashamed to admit it," says Deeb. "I'm crazy about the Three Stooges." He adds, "there seems to be some truth to the belief that they were vastly underrated throughout their long career."

Newspaper articles on the Stooges have popped up quite frequently recently, stemming primarily from yet another media phenomenon. Recently many television stations have been scheduling broadcast of the Stooges comedies for late-night viewing, in what is generally considered an "adult" time slot. As a result, many of the people who "grew up" with the Stooges, by watching them on afternoon television in the late 1950s and early '60s, have renewed their interest in the team. Many of them, like Gary Deeb, have come to enjoy them even more as adults.

While the Three Stooges have recently been a

topic of discussion in the print media, actual Three Stooges film festivals are growing in number and popularity as well. This is in itself a phenomenon, considering the fact that their old movies are so often played, and have been played for so long, on television. Chicago audiences, for example, have seen the Stooges comedies almost continuously since 1958, when independent WGN Television began airing them as part of a weekday noontime children's program. Later, the time slot was changed to late afternoon, afterschool hours, hosted by Chicago television personality Bob Bell. Set in the "Odeon Theater," Bell introduced the shorts, read letters from viewers, and occasionally warned children of the hazards of practicing Stooges slapsticks on their friends. Eventually WGN dropped the afternoon Stooges showings, but continued to broadcast the shorts on Saturday mornings. Presented along with Laurel and Hardy and Abbott and Costello cartoons, the Stooges comedies became part of the "Funny Men" for several years until WGN dropped the Stooges from their lineup completely.

Another local Chicago station, WFLD, almost immediately picked up the shorts and began running them in an hour-long time slot each weekday afternoon. The old movies enhanced WFLD's ratings considerably, and the independent station played them to the hilt. In addition to weekday afternoon broadcast, the Stooges showings were expanded to include Saturday and Sunday presentations. Eventually the Stooges shorts found themselves occupying late evening weekday time periods on WFLD, with additional scheduling of the films during the early morning hours as well.

Other stations throughout the country have had considerable success with the Columbia shorts. Local independent stations in all of the major cities have included the Stooges comedies as part of their weekday afternoon programming schedules. In addition, the stations have often played the comedies during prime time or late-evening hours. The Columbia Stooges shorts are also becoming a popular item on cable television, where they are shown uncut and without commercial interruption.

Because of the demand for "Three Stooges" programming, attempts to resurrect their style of comedy have continued even today. Norman Maurer recently produced a series of Three Stooges cartoons for CBS television, and has churned out a number of Stooges-related products as well. Three Stooges novelty items have increased in popularity over the years.

Another recent idea capitalizing on the popularity of the Three Stooges is the Three Stooges "Fan Club." Morris Feinberg, Larry Fine's brother, is president of the club, which is headquartered in his home town of Philadelphia. Feinberg publishes several club newsletters each year, keeping fans up to date on the latest film festivals and activities, as well as publishing articles from contributing writers about the Stooges.

The public affection and admiration for the Three Stooges has not diminished since Moe Howard's death several years ago. If anything, it has actually increased. The Three Stooges are quickly becoming our nation's most revered clowns, something that the Stooges themselves thought would never happen.

"When we were on top," said Moe in a newspaper interview, "nobody liked me. After all, I'm the mean one who does all the hitting. Now the kids come up to me on the street and say they love me. I can't figure it out. A couple of new generations popped up while we had our back turned and they're different, I guess." Different, perhaps, but loyal fans nevertheless.

Although all of the original "Three Stooges" are gone, the impact their comedy had on the American motion picture will not quickly be erased. They were the most prolific comedy team in the history of movies, and they proved themselves to be the most durable. They survived when others dropped into obscurity and reached new heights of popularity when slapstick was almost considered a dirty word. And they created a brand of violent physical comedy that will not soon be forgotten. It is this style of comedy that singles out the Three Stooges as one of the most unusual, and controversial, acts in the history of screen comedy.

The Three Stooges never achieved widespread critical acceptance, at least not during their time. As long as pretensions against comedy for comedy's sake exist, they never will.

In retrospect, however, the Three Stooges accomplished exactly what they had always intended to do.

They made people laugh.